MW01530534

SEEING RED

Seeing Red

A Novel

Shawn Sutherland

$| N_1 | O_2 | N_1$
CANADA

Copyright © 2014 by Shawn Sutherland

All rights reserved. No part of this book may be used or reproduced
in any manner whatsoever without the prior written permission of the publisher,
except in the case of brief quotations embodied in reviews.

*Publisher's note: This book is a work of fiction. Names, characters, places and
incidents are either the product of the author's imagination or are used
fictitiously, and any resemblance to actual persons living or dead
is entirely coincidental.*

Library and Archives Canada Cataloguing in Publication

Sutherland, Shawn, 1985–, author
Seeing red / Shawn Sutherland.

ISBN 978–1–926942–75–9 (pbk.)

I. Title.

PS8637.U864S43 2014   C813'.6   C2014–904747–9

Printed and bound in Canada on 100% recycled paper.

Now Or Never Publishing
#313, 1255 Seymour Street
Vancouver, British Columbia
Canada V6B 0H1

nonpublishing.com
Fighting Words.

We acknowledge the support of the Canada Council
for the Arts for our publishing program.

—Part i—

En Bloc Party

ONE

The blackouts started shortly after I arrived in Toronto. I typ-ically spent the night hunched over a bar counter, sipping scotch on the rocks and making small talk with the regulars before waking up hours later in an unfamiliar place with no rec-ollection as to why I was there. I'd open my eyes to find myself lying on a park bench, a stoop in a dark alleyway, or in a woman's bedroom on the other side of town. It was easier in those days, a year ago, when I didn't know anybody. I could drink as much as I wanted to with no fear of reprisal, no consequence. I spoke exclusively to strangers and kept the conversation on the surface. Names, faces—they were all interchangeable to me.

When I first came to the city in the summer of '09, I had nothing. The apartment was empty: no bed, no furniture, they didn't even leave me a shower curtain. Just hardwood floors and a balcony overlooking the streets. I threw pillows and blankets down in the centre of the room and slept there, passing the time by reading novels, perusing through the phonebook and setting up appointments to have the cable installed or a futon delivered. Nobody knew I was there, separated from the world, and the hours passed slowly.

Resting downstairs in the parking garage, my rusted black '98 Cavalier, a car I affectionately nicknamed "The Widowmaker," was loaded to the brim with everything I owned: mostly clothes, books, silverware and small appliances. I gradual-ly unloaded the car piece by piece, lugging boxes up and down the elevator again and again. On one occasion, I ran into a frail elderly man originally from India. He had awful posture—his legs and torso met at a ninety-degree angle—and yet he offered to help me move as he welcomed me into the building. I smiled and politely declined. Another woman held the elevator door open for me as I awkwardly tried to balance a box full of dishes. She had just purchased a big flatscreen TV and was excited to tell me all about it. The people in Toronto had a bad reputation—all my life I had heard they were rude and cold—but these tenants seemed more than friendly enough.

The apartment looked sterile and desolate, like a hospital room, even after I finished unpacking. I didn't have any pictures or paintings to hang on the walls because I wasn't accustomed to staying in one place for very long. My father had died three years earlier and I used the money he left me to live like a vagrant, driving from place to place and working odd jobs while attending various post-secondary schools. By that time I had already spent thousands upon thousands of dollars on tuition fees and bar tabs and my savings were disappearing fast. To keep my cost of living low I often rented rooms in dingy basement apartments, and by doing so I was able to allocate more money to beer, gin, rum, wine—whatever I could get my hands on at the time. My daily routine consisted of sleeping until noon, drinking two cans of beer in the shower, attending a lecture, opening a bottle of liquor after class and then frequenting the pubs at night, where I sat and drank and waited for something, anything, to happen.

That's how it was for me. I'd arrive in town with no contacts and no place to stay, then gradually meet the locals, make a few acquaintances, wear out my welcome and move onto the next place, transferring school credits and burning bridges wherever I went. I was alone during the holidays. I did everything alone. I remained in contact with no one—save for one girl.

But Toronto was going to be different. I had grown tired of the aimless drifting and the meaningless, half-hour friendships and decided to draw a line in the sand. I envisioned myself getting a journalism degree and a job at a local newspaper and then settling down and sobering up once and for all. I was only twenty-three years old, but I knew exactly what I wanted. The goal was simple. My plans were derailed, however, when I received a phone call at three o'clock in the morning a few days after moving in. It was from an old friend, one I hadn't spoken to in a long time, so

I knew it was important. And after I hung up the phone that night, I immediately reverted back into old habits.

There were never any slow nights. Even on a Tuesday—typically the worst night of the week for social drinking—I could find people willing to binge. And so we did. The city allowed me to indulge in my aberrant lifestyle to an extent I had never experienced before. I became addicted to it. And, as time went on, my alcohol-induced amnesia gradually progressed until weeks and months seemed to disappear altogether, like a dream that fades soon after you wake.

It was perfect.

Two

Somebody told me one time that once you've lived here long enough, your mind begins to tune out the noise. Humming traffic, sirens echoing in the distance, recycled air spewing in and out of the sewers and skyscrapers—it all conflates into a hollow silence. It's comforting, and I could probably sleep here for several hours were it not for the cool breeze blowing against my face. As I gradually open my eyes, I realize I'm lying on a patch of artificial grass on the rooftop of an old two-storey building.

Judging by the sun it's around six o'clock in the morning. I slowly lift my head off the grass to see a small garden with an adjacent wooden patio. There are empty beer bottles, metal kegs, cigarette butts, pieces of clothing and red plastic cups strewn all over the roof. No sign of anyone else. It's July 2010 and I'm wearing nothing more than a pair of brown shoes, grey jeans and a black t-shirt with the Brian Jonestown Massacre logo on the front. Climbing to my feet I see the CN Tower looming in the distance, and with the sun rising in the background it looks like the scene off a postcard. A faint taste of liquor still lingers in the back of my throat, the daylight hurts my eyes and my head is throbbing. I have no memory of the night before—only subtle glimpses, transparent faces and a vague recollection of the words I might have said.

The silver hip flask in my back pocket has remnants of gin left in it. I take a short sip and it burns away the morning grime on my teeth and my lips, and then I exhale and wipe my mouth. As my hand pulls away, I notice a patch of dry blood on the last two knuckles. Could be mine, could be from someone else. There's also writing on my left forearm. The name *Jody*—along with her phone number—has been scribbled onto the skin with a black magic marker. Definitely not my handwriting. Underneath it reads: "Call her! She's really nice!"

I'm probably not going to call her.

I have only a brief moment to orient myself before the phone in my pocket begins to vibrate. I check the display to see it's Jeff Dockett, a former classmate and current drinking buddy of mine. He's a crude, abrasive, frat-boy prick, but for some reason we seem to get along. You can't explain chemistry. We met in the fall of last year while we were both taking a survey course at Ryerson University. He was majoring in business and I was studying journalism. Why, I don't know—I no longer had any intention of becoming a journalist. Maybe I was just so used to being in school that I didn't know how to function outside of it. School is safe, familiar. You can hide at the back of a lecture hall and go completely unnoticed. And they let you choose your own schedule— I always ensure my classes are held in the afternoon so I can sleep off the hangovers.

Anyway, one day I ran into "Doc" at the campus pub when we were supposed to be in class and discovered he shared a similar penchant for hard liquor. I had seen him on campus prior to that, but never thought much of it; he had a tendency to wear big sweaters and brand new baseball caps and he seemed far too confident and outgoing for my liking. However, that afternoon, he pulled up a stool next to me and proceeded to order glass after glass of whiskey. Perhaps I'd underestimated the man. Eventually we struck up a conversation, and from that point on we became the best of friends. He was the catalyst for my social life in the city, the kind of person who seemed to know everybody. I met several people through him and now I had friends to drink with on the weekends—I only drank alone during the week.

"Hey," I mutter into the phone. My voice is stale and raspy.

"Ethan! What's up, man? We just landed. How far away are you?"

I remember it now: I was supposed to pick Doc up from the airport. He had flown in on the red-eye from Vancouver and needed a ride home. I check my watch. The battery is dead. The hands aren't moving. I tap it with my index finger and nothing happens.

"Oh, I'll be there . . . any second now."

"You haven't even left yet, have you?"

"Not yet."

"Man, you sound like complete dog shit! And your phone keeps echoing. I can hear everything you say twice."

"I bet it sounds even better the second time," I say, coughing hoarsely.

"Did you go out again last night?"

"Yeah."

"Where?"

"I don't know."

"You *don't know?*"

"Never mind. I'll be there soon. Just . . . sit tight."

"Hurry! I'm fuckin' tired. I didn't sleep at all on the plane. There was this kid whining in front of me, and I was like, 'Shut up, kid!' I was kicking his seat and shit."

"Did it work?"

"Nah, it just upset him more."

"Huh. So, how was Vancouver?" I ask, scanning the rooftop for an exit. Doc had been visiting his older sister Kelly to congratulate her on delivering a baby boy the week before. While not particularly interested in meeting the newest member of his family, Doc jumped at the opportunity to go on a trip and get drunk and embarrass himself in a whole new city.

"Oh man, it was awesome. Got to meet my new nephew! He's an ugly, *ugly* looking kid though. He just looks . . . terrible."

I can't help but laugh. Doc speaks without a trace of malice in his voice, so he can usually get away with saying things most of us can't, no matter how offensive. People just accept it like they would from a small child. I prefer to have friends who don't sugarcoat the truth anyway. It's better than being lied to.

"That's too bad," I deadpan. "I was hoping he'd be really good looking."

"Nope! Must skip a generation. Anyway, I'll tell you more when you get here. Hurry!"

"Okay, I'm leaving now."

I hang up the phone and gather my bearings while staring out at the skyline. Despite the constant hum, the stagnant noise, the city looks peaceful. No swirling lights or gaudy signs, no people shouting or music blaring. Just a cool breeze and the small onset of sunlight peering over the horizon. I gaze at the downtown core and wish it could always look this peaceful; that I could enjoy all the benefits of this mass urban collective without the crowded sidewalks, the herds, the shoulder-to-shoulder transit rides, without cramming onto elevators or standing in line. I wish I could walk down the middle of Yonge Street and scream as loudly as possible and hear nothing but the sound of my own voice reverberating off the buildings. I always appreciate mornings like these because I come across them so rarely. Watching the city rise before anyone else—that's something to be savoured.

There's an open hatch at the far end of the patio across from a crudely written sign that reads: *Fuck with the garden, and the garden fucks with you!* I make a mental note not to fuck with the garden and carefully climb down a ladder leading to the top of a wooden staircase. The interior of the building looks and smells like sawdust and every door is locked shut. With nowhere else to go, I descend the stairs and walk out onto the street.

Searching the neighbourhood, I find the Widowmaker abandoned beside an old yellow church, sheltered beneath a row of maple trees. A taxi speeds around the curb and nearly barrels into me, but I barely notice because I'm fixated on a fresh crack in the windshield—a small, white spiderweb on the upper-left corner. Somebody must have thrown a rock at it last night. I unlock the door and slump down into the seat only to realize that the window on the passenger side has been completely smashed and there are shards of glass all over the floor. My iPod is also missing; the cord is still plugged into the auxiliary port of the car radio, but the unit itself is gone.

"Goddammit!" I shout, hitting the steering wheel with the palm of my hand. Technically this isn't even my car anymore; I sold it to Dockett months ago. Living in the city, with access to buses, subways and streetcars, I didn't see the need to own a vehicle anymore—besides, gas and insurance prices were too high. But I was reluctant to sell it to a complete stranger, unwilling to part with it entirely. The old bucket of bolts had sentimental value and we had traveled far and well together. I'd slept in the backseat on more than one occasion—not exactly the Hilton, but it sufficed. While he was away, Doc lent me the keys on the sole condition that I provide him with a ride to and from the airport. It felt good to be behind the wheel again. Like seeing an old friend.

I kick the remaining pieces of glass out onto the pavement, then start the engine and put it in gear and navigate through the streets of downtown Toronto toward the Gardiner Expressway. The wind blows furiously through the missing window, my eyesight is still foggy from the night before and traffic lights seem to have a fourth dimension to them. Admittedly, I'm too hungover to be driving, but the inner city roads are sluggish and the odds of a fatal collision are relatively low. Still, I'm overwhelmed by the urge to recline in my seat and sleep it off for a few hours, despite already being late. I put on a pair of sunglasses to ease the burning sensation in my eyes and then turn up the radio to drown out the noise from the window. It's set to a college station playing indie rock music from the nineties—the last decade before everything turned to shit. An indifferent singer pines for a girl over oddly-tuned guitars and understated drum beats. I like it. *From now on, I can see the sun. Makes me nervous, makes me run.*

More cars and trucks appear seemingly out of thin air as I merge onto the 427. The traffic becomes stagnant and congested and the big SUV behind me nearly touches my rear bumper. "Stop tailgating, you asshole!" I yell into the mirror. During a commercial break, I switch the radio over to classic rock playing the same old songs they've had in their rotation for the past forty years. I know all the lyrics, even those of the songs I hate, and when the opening riff to "Pretty Woman" starts pouring through the speakers I immediately turn it off. That song is a repetitive piece of shit. Without music, I can hear the engines and the screeching of tires and an occasional honk and I feel the pressure against my temple with every pulse of sound. Gridlock. The city has awoken. The tranquility and solitude I experienced only minutes ago is long dead. The pawns, the sheep, they're all awake.

I follow the airport signs to the arrivals section where I find Doc sitting on the curb next to a row of idle cabs. He's wearing a red plaid shirt and a black baseball cap turned backwards, and he has one hell of a scowl on his face. I pull up beside him and he angrily opens the passenger side door. "Took you long enough!" he growls, tossing his bag into the backseat. As we're driving away, he tries to roll up the window, but nothing happens.

"What the hell?"

"That's weird. It was there a minute ago."

"You broke my window? How?" He looks down at my forearm. "And who the fuck is *Jody*?"

Doc complains throughout the entire drive back into the city, alternating between cursing at me and muttering to himself. He tells me stories about his exploits in Vancouver and then interrupts his own anecdotes just to swear at me some more, calling me a retard and a piece of shit and a fuck-face for breaking his window. Gusts of air hit him directly in the eyes as we speed down the highway and he awkwardly tries to block the wind with his hands, but to no avail.

"Look, I'm sorry. I'll pay for it," I tell him, and he shakes his head. "Hey, believe me, I'm pissed off too. They stole my iPod. Now how am I supposed to listen to Whitesnake?"

"Just . . . just get me home. You bring the booze tonight and we'll call it even. But I'm warning you, I'm gonna be drinking a *lot*. Like shit-faced, puking, pissing-all-over-myself drunk. You in?"

"Wouldn't miss it for the world."

"Good. I told Craig and Scott to show up around eight."

No surprise there. The four of us drink together every weekend without fail. Today is Friday, so we'll go to Dockett's apartment and stock his fridge full of alcohol and then laugh and play cards until we're sufficiently inebriated. Then we'll frequent the bars, the seedy clubs, and awkwardly talk to women. Sometimes some of us get lucky. Most of the time we don't. But that's the game and we play it every goddamn weekend.

"Sounds good," I say, fiddling with the knobs on the radio. "I have a few errands to run, but I'll come by after."

"What kinda errands?"

"Oh, you know. The usual."

THREE

Later that day, I find myself sitting alone in a doctor's office at the walk-in clinic waiting for him or her to enter the room. The walls are pure white and covered in the usual motif: diagrams of the circulatory system, anti-smoking ads with black lungs and rotten teeth, cartoon germs professing the dangers of not washing your hands. I leisurely scan the room to see if there's anything worth stealing. Not that I would—it's just a game to pass the time. Aside from a jar full of cotton swabs and some rubbing alcohol, it looks like slim pickings. Maybe there's something in the desk drawer? Probably not. These walk-in clinics are usually pretty cheap.

A few minutes pass before a grey-haired man wearing a long white coat suddenly comes in through the door. He sits at a small chair at a small desk and gives me the requisite small talk before asking, "So, Mr. Reid, what can I do for you today?" I'm not sure where to begin. How do you describe it? It would take hours to fully explain my condition.

"Lately, I've been getting these blackouts," I tell him. "Memory lapses."

"Uh huh. And when do these lapses occur?" he asks me with his head held down, leisurely writing into an open folder.

"Well, it's like last night. I drank no more than I usually do, and yet I can't remember a single thing. After a certain point it all cuts out."

"Uh huh. And how much do you typically drink in one night?"

"It depends. I know I had some gin. . . ."

"Anything else?"

"Maybe a little scotch, too."

"And then you blacked out?"

"No, that was before I left the apartment."

"Okay, so where did you go?"

"I drove to this bar somewhere on Queen Street and drank there for a few hours. Then I met this girl and she invited me to a rooftop party. I found the receipt in my back pocket, so I know I had about twelve drinks, two shots of whiskey, some . . . chicken wings. . . ."

Now I have his attention. He closes the folder and leans toward me. "This is a typical night for you?"

"Yeah. It's never been a problem before."

"How long have you been drinking like this?"

"Since I was seventeen."

"How often?"

"Almost every day."

"And how old are you now?"

"Twenty-four."

He nods and stares down at the floor before continuing: "Well, severe amnesia can occur when there's a deficiency of Vitamin B1 in the brain caused by excessive alcohol consumption. We had a guy in here one time who had what's called 'Korsakoff's Syndrome.' He couldn't remember a thing. You wouldn't be at that stage yet. You're far too young. I think it's more likely that your body is simply getting older, wearing down. It can't process as much as it used to."

"Isn't there anything I can do? I mean, sometimes I run into people on the street and they recognize me and talk to me, like they know everything about me, but I have absolutely *no idea* who they are. Or I wake up and there's blood on my hands. One time,

I got out of bed and the furniture in my apartment had been completely rearranged. Badly, too. No feng shui involved whatsoever—"

I could go on, but he stops me. "Let's take a look at you." I move from the chair to the exam table and he does a full body checkup: first the ears, then the throat and the eyes. Spends a lot of time on the eyes. "No signs of jaundice," he explains. Then he stops for a moment while examining my face. "When did you break your nose?"

"Huh?"

"You have a slightly deviated septum."

"Oh. Probably from getting punched in the face. Can they fix that?"

"No, not without surgery. And that's movie star stuff. I wouldn't recommend it unless it's obstructing your breathing."

My shirt comes off and the stethoscope comes out. I lie down on the table and he listens to my heart, my lungs and my abdomen while telling me to breathe in and out several times. Satisfied, he puts the stethoscope away. "You seem fine. Healthy as a horse."

"I do take a lot of vitamins."

"Hmm. It doesn't seem like there's anything *physically* wrong with you, at least not at this point. We'll have to do a blood test to see if there's any cirrhosis of the liver. In the meantime, the only thing I can recommend is that you abstain from alcohol for a little while. Perhaps look into counseling."

Granted, there are some things in my life I'd rather forget, but the notion of completely losing control on a nightly basis is a tad unnerving. I was hoping for a prescription, a pill, something that would allow me to maintain my current lifestyle without the blackouts. Drink less? That's his answer? Get fucking real. And counseling? I don't have the time or the patience to lie on a couch and field questions from some old prick who doesn't know what it's like. Maybe I should just buy some Vitamin B1 and see if that helps.

"If the problem persists, make an appointment and we'll do some more testing. But I should warn you: if you keep drinking like this, your body is eventually going to break down. Not only your brain, but your liver, your kidneys, everything."

"How long do I have?" I ask cryptically.

He pauses and stares at me blankly. "If you don't stop? I'd say another twenty, thirty years."

"*Fuck*," I whisper.

"Why don't you try taking a week off and see how you feel?"

The doctor flashes me a phony smile and pats me on the shoulder as he hands me a business card. He tells me to call him if I run into any trouble and says he'll recommend a good counselor for me to talk to. That's the problem with these walk-in clinics: sure, they're free and you don't have to make an appointment, but they offer only band-aid solutions. The doctor and I talk a little more about my anxiety attacks and frequent chest pains and he suggests I stop eating red meat because the cows are pumped full of hormones. Then he writes me a prescription for an anti-anxiety drug, one I've tried before. It didn't work. He explains the proper dosage and side effects and I thank him and then leave the clinic, crumpling up the prescription and tossing it into the trash on my way out.

Later, after a brief trip to the liquor store, I'm standing in front of my apartment door in a hallway with a crooked ceiling and stained blue carpeting. Inside, the place is a mess: empty beer and liquor bottles line the floor alongside a tower of discarded pizza boxes and overflowing garbage bags. There are dirty dishes in the sink, clothes strewn all over the furniture and burnt-out light bulbs that need to be replaced. Still no pictures or paintings on the walls. I take off my shoes and my shirt and walk into the bathroom and open the cabinet behind the mirror. On the shelf sit several vitamin supplements, cough medicines and little orange bottles with white lids filled with prescription drugs. I go through each bottle and pour pills into the palm of my right hand until there's a large pile. Then I run the cold water and pop the capsules into my mouth and drink from the stream and swallow. Vitamins A, C, D, E, calcium, magnesium and zinc to keep my body functioning. I also take glutamine and probiotics because my gut is no doubt damaged from all the alcohol.

I want to take a long nap. The last bottle on the bottom shelf contains extra strength melatonin. I place three circular pills in my mouth and let them dissolve beneath my tongue. They taste like breath mints. Stumbling out of the bathroom, I draw the window shades to prevent the light from getting in, then remove the rest of my clothes and collapse into bed, not to wake again until the early evening. With melatonin, my dreams are more vivid, more real, and I dream that I'm younger, surrounded by family, and that the world is still small.

FOUR

City life is hard on the knees. The streets are laden with jagged pavement and concrete. You rely on the subway: a shaky train that wobbles and sways while your legs twist like screws, grinding the cartilage in your joints. It squeals along the track and stops and starts and you depart the car but it's not over yet: a mad rush leaves alongside you, each person shuffling to the exit like they're escaping a fire, and they push and squeeze together as they march up several flights of rigid stairs to the streets above. It's nothing like Ezra Pound described. There are no goddamn petals. I've only lived here for a year, but with every step there's a sharp, stinging pain between my kneecap and femur bone. Luckily, there's a pill for that: glucosamine is said to take the pain away in as little as six weeks. I take two daily with meals.

Tonight, however, the southbound train ride en route to Doc's apartment is relatively stress-free. Several passengers get off at Bloor Station and I actually manage to find a seat. To my left, two people are hunched over with their heads held down, gazing at their cellphones and clicking and reading and typing text messages with both hands. Always texting. The sheep love to text. I heard in London they actually had to cover lampposts in foam padding because too many idiots, immersed in gadgetry, were walking straight into them. To my right, two friends are standing side by side, one wearing a long dark coat and staring at the Blackberry in his hand and the other dressed head to toe in

Reebok athletic attire and leaning against a pole while spouting off a one-way conversation. I can't help but overhear him say, "So, I've started to play basketball more *intensely*. For exercise, y'know? But, my left knee, it's like, kinda broken. So, it's normally okay, but it starts to hurt if I walk for a long period of time. Or if I play basketball *intensely*. Or if I dance."

People say stupid, asinine shit like this all the time. In every coffee shop, in every convenience store, on every street corner, you hear snippets of it. In the city, you're surrounded by it: a constant reminder that my generation is sleepwalking through life, gorging on reality TV and vacantly watching silly cats on YouTube with our eyes permanently fixated on little rectangular screens. We play it safe, avoid conflict, end our relationships via text message because we're afraid of phone calls and we brush our teeth before going to the dentist and then lie about how often we floss just so we don't get scolded. We communicate with each other in mono-syllabic grunts and moans and chuckle like troglodytes all while steering clear of any debate or meaningful conversation. None of us read or vote or protest or give a shit about anything that actu-ally matters. Everything we do—it's all so meaningless.

Our generation doesn't even have a proper name. I've heard them call us Generation Y, Echo Boomers, Millennials, but the name never sticks. Why? Because no single name can define us. We aren't unified by *anything*. Our taste in music, entertainment, politics, it's all over the map, so it's hard to find any common ground. We have no shared identity, no causes to rally behind, no sense of community, and as a result it's easy to feel disconnected. Alienated. Completely lost in the shuffle.

My eyes gradually wander upward to the subway map: an illustration of yellow, green and blue intersecting lines set against a black background. There's a short purple line, too, but nobody cares about that one. Kiping Station to the left, McCowan Station to the right. A yellow line for Yonge and a green line for Bloor. The blue line leads into Scarborough, the east side of Toronto. I've only been there once. Now, whenever I look at it, I think of Rachael Burke.

A long time ago, when I was eighteen, I rode the train into Union Station and met her there, somewhere inside the colossal main hall. She was wearing a fluffy pink sweater—I remember it clearly—and when she spotted me her face lit up and she ran across the hall and jumped into my arms. She told me she had gotten lost in the station and had to ask a transit employee for directions and he chaperoned her there. Then she smiled and waved to him as we walked downstairs. I told her I was happy to see her again. At the time, she was living in Scarborough, so we rode the subway across the entire blue line back to her place. We laughed and caught up and I recited stories about my new job delivering Chinese food to rich people by the lakeshore and she told me about her classes at UTSC and the pet rabbit she wanted to buy. I haven't been on the blue line since that day. Hard to believe it was almost seven years ago.

The train comes to a halt and I arduously march up the stairs until my knees are killing me. Thankfully, Doc lives only a short walk away from Dundas Station. His place is a palace compared to mine, with large windows, an open-concept kitchen and fresh IKEA furniture, all paid for by his well-to-do parents. His father works as a defence contractor, designing and selling warships for the military or something like that. I've never gotten a straight answer out of him. Whatever he does, it must pay well. Doc knows that one day he'll inherit his father's money, which affords him the opportunity to waste time taking random business courses with little concern for the future. I wish I had that same golden parachute waiting for me, but alas, I don't.

A stranger kindly holds the security door open for me as I walk into the lobby. I nod at the concierge who recognizes me and then ride the elevator up to the fifth floor. The door is unlocked, so I enter unannounced. Doc is sprawled out on a leather couch with his feet resting on a coffee table, watching baseball on TV while clutching a can of Budweiser. I drop a paper bag full of liquor onto the black granite countertop and help myself to some ice in the fridge and then pour a scotch on the rocks before lazing on the other side of the couch.

"Hey," he says.

"What's up."

"The Jays are losing to Boston. Three-nothing."

"Fuck."

"I know."

"Ah, baseball's a flakey game."

"This is true."

"No sign of the others?"

"They said they'll be here in, like, an hour."

"Cool."

The game cuts to a commercial break, and advertisements for sneakers, luxury sedans and Old Spice deodorant flash across the screen.

"So, any luck with the job hunt?" he asks.

"I didn't really look this week. Nobody's called me back either."

"You should've just stayed at that call centre."

"No way. I couldn't. That place was soul-destroying."

I recently quit my job at a telecommunications firm where I earned minimum wage providing technical support for people having trouble with their cellphones. The calls came in from Alabama, Louisiana, Georgia and Texas, so I was yelled at by angry rednecks all day long. That was my job. For every call, you'd have to repeat the same company-approved introduction, closing statement, and let the customer know that *we appreciate their business* at some point in the conversation. If you failed to do so, a supervisor would immediately appear over your shoulder to scold you. They also forced us to act sympathetic, to tell the customer how frustrated we were by their problem and how we would do everything in our power to fix it. It was all so rehearsed, so fake. And mind-numbing. I looked around at the people who had been working at that same job for ten years without a promotion and wondered how they did it. Their eyes seemed glazed over; like veterans of war, they had that blank, thousand-yard stare. I probably would've blown my brains out within the first eight months.

"But yeah," I continue, "I thought I'd find another job by now."

"Nah, you won't find shit because your résumé sucks ass."

"It's not that bad! I mean, I don't have a lot of experience, but how the hell am I supposed to get any if no one's gonna hire me?"

"You should take a look at mine. It's on the desktop." With his eyes still focused on the game, he lifts his arm and lazily flails his wrist toward the computer on the far side of the room. I grudgingly get up from the couch and take a seat at the black IKEA computer desk. The deep space-themed screensaver stops when I move the mouse and the password prompt pops up.

"What's your password?"

"Huh?"

"Password!"

"Knifetits."

I think I misheard him. "What?"

"KNIFETITS!" he yells. "All one word."

I type it in and press *Enter* and it works. Windows takes over a minute to load and then I see a file on the desktop called "Big Resume." I open it up and print it off and bring a paper copy back to the couch. The first thing I notice is the header: his name, Jeffrey Dockett, is not only written in an elaborate, serpentine font, but it's also underlined and accounts for nearly a third of the page. Everything else is written in capital letters.

"It says here you speak French?"

"Bonjour, allo, salut, motherfucker."

"And under a subheading called *Strengths*, you wrote: 'I'm a real live wire who plays hard and fast with the rules and can't get out of his own way.' "

"Yeah! They want people who take initiative."

"And this is how you got hired at Starbucks?"

Doc has been working at Starbucks for the past two months—at his parents' insistence. While they pay his rent, tuition, phone, cable and car insurance bills, they demand he earn his own disposable income. Doc refers to this income as *burn money* and he spends it as soon as he makes it. We all do. Nobody can afford to save these days.

"Yeah, man!" he says. "They love me there."

"Well, I don't know why they'd ever hire you." Then I hold up his résumé and shake it in front of him. "This is a real piece of shit."

"Ah, land of the blind."

"What?"

" 'In the land of the blind, the one-eyed man is king.' Ever heard that?"

"Yeah, but—"

"Some people think it's about being disabled, or a cyclops or some shit, but it's not. It's about *mediocrity*. It means: you don't have to be *good*, you just have to be better than those *around* you. It's like with school. You don't have to get a hundred percent on every test, you just have to score higher than the other people in your class, which usually isn't all that hard. If everybody around you is blind, then all you need is one eye open. Not two."

"Okay, but how does that apply here?"

Doc shrugs his shoulders. "I'm not the most qualified person in the world, but I'm still better than all those other assholes who applied that week." Then he belches and cracks open another can of Budweiser and slurps the froth as it rises over the tab. "Plus, I'm willing to work the morning shift."

"How do you like being a barista, by the way?"

"Don't call it that. Sounds girly."

"What do you call it then?"

He considers for a moment. "I'm a *coffee man*."

"Okay, how do you like being a 'coffee man'?"

"Ah, a job's a job. Tomorrow's my last shift until Wednesday. Heading up to the cottage on Sunday. Should be good."

"Don't you have to work at, like, five o'clock in the morning some days? I don't know how you do that."

He shrugs his shoulders again. "A job's a job."

FIVE

The global recession hit us hard in 2010. It was difficult to find work—especially for young people my age with no discernible skills or motivation—and any job you were lucky enough to get came with fewer hours and less pay. The North American post-war gold rush of the previous century was long over. The manufacturing sector had shut down and moved overseas. We didn't make things anymore, we just shuffled money around.

In June, I woke up early every morning to be out pounding the pavement by 10AM. There were no *Help Wanted* signs on the commercial streets, the one exception being an independent coffee shop with a poster in the window advertising part-time work. When I went inside to drop off a résumé, the old Asian lady behind the counter informed me, in broken English, that she would only hire a female. I walked through shopping malls and received a similar reaction everywhere I went: some managers took my résumé and politely feigned interest, asking questions like "Do you have any experience in retail?" while scribbling indiscernible notes at the top of the page, but I never received a single call from any of the people I met, nor did any of them try to schedule an interview.

As I was leaving the mall I decided to try my luck at one last place, a record store that also sold DVDs and video games. I asked the girl behind the counter to fetch me a manager and she sighed and told me I was the fifth or sixth person to come in looking for a job that day.

"How were the other applicants?" I asked.

"Ah, they seemed alright," she said.

"*Shit*," I mumbled. She smiled at that. Moments later I was greeted by a large, greasy man with shoulder-length hair and a dirty Iron Maiden t-shirt. These days, men like this exist by the millions: poor bedeviled guys leading sad, pointless lives played out on computer screens, experiencing the world from the comfort of their own reclining chairs. Yet, somehow, this man had a managerial job and I didn't. How does that happen? I think the key is to spend enough time in one place working for the same company and you'll eventually climb the ladder to a mid-level position. Unfortunately, I've never had the patience to do that. I told him I was looking for work and he fed me the familiar line of questioning; I smiled from ear to ear and tried to answer with that phony, bullshit workplace enthusiasm.

"Full or part-time?" he asked.

"Preferably full-time, but I'd be happy with either."

"Do you like movies?"

What did he expect me to say to that? *No. Don't care for movies. Never seen a good one. They're all bad.*

"Oh yes. I've seen several."

"What about music?"

"Love music. I used to play in bands when I was a teenager."

"What kind of music do you like?"

"Indie rock and punk, mostly, but I run the gamut. I like folk music and old blues from the forties and fifties, like Sonny Boy Williamson and Son House to—"

"Like video games?" he interrupted.

"Oh yeah. Still play them often. I have an Xbox and PlayStation and I used to own every Nintendo console."

"Cool."

"And your name is?"

"Louis."

I shook his hand. "Thanks, Louis. It was nice meeting you."

I left the store. Louis never called. Neither did any of the other managers who made notes on my résumé that day. Apparently, even though I'm young, enthusiastic and university-educated, I'm not qualified to sell CDs at the mall.

A few weeks earlier, I had an interview with the owner of a Second Cup coffee shop. I had been drinking heavily the night before and didn't sleep very well—my eyes were bloodshot and my mind felt hazy. The owner was a clean-cut man with a pressed black shirt, black tie, short black hair and a lazy left eye. Probably in his early thirties. We sat uncomfortably close to each other in a cramped booth and he asked me about my résumé, my work experience, what I had studied in school and why I wanted to work in a coffee shop. Everything was going well until he wanted to know what kind of coffee I liked. I scrambled to think of an answer because I rarely drink coffee. I was also very, very hungover.

"Uh . . . black? Sometimes I put a little cream in there, though, and stir it up. I like, uh, Maxwell House? But, to tell you the truth, I'm more of a tea-drinker. Can't get enough of that tea in the morning."

"What kind of tea?"

"Uh . . . black?"

He stared at me with a confused look on his face. At that point I realized I probably should have done a little research on coffee and tea before agreeing to the interview. Five minutes on the internet really could have helped me.

"Cool. So. Ethan. Tell me. Why should I hire you?" I was slightly taken aback because interviewers usually aren't so direct. Again I had to improvise.

"Well, I'm a hard worker. I'm loyal and I'm . . . totally punctual—"

He interrupted me. "No, no, no, cut the *bullshit!* I want to know the real you. Like, say, when you go to a party, what do you like to drink?"

I was stunned. Was he hitting on me? No, he couldn't be. But then no interviewer had ever called me on my bullshit before or inquired about my drinking preferences. I was unsure as to how much information to divulge; nobody wants to hire an alcoholic, but I had to give him something.

"Umm, I'm not much of a drinker, to be honest, but if I did have one, I'd probably order a scotch on the rocks. Maybe a gin-and-tonic."

"Right on," he said with a smile. He seemed satisfied by my answer. Then he began to describe what the job entailed and the hours I'd be expected to work. He said he could only offer me about sixteen hours per week, usually on Saturday and Sunday mornings at 5:30AM, probably because those were the shifts nobody else wanted-ed. They would pay me minimum wage plus a cut of whatever change was left in the tip jar, which would amount to an extra buck or two. I was also expected to clean the bathroom sink and scrub the shit off the toilet at least once per shift. As he droned on, my eyes began to burn and I struggled to keep them open until I hit a breaking point and couldn't continue the charade any longer.

"I'm sorry, man," I interrupted. "But that all sounds *terrible*."

"You don't want the job?"

"No. I mean, I do, but . . ." My voice trailed off.

"Are you okay?"

"Too much *scotch* last night!" I admitted. "I should probably go home and lie down."

He nodded and we sat in awkward silence for about five seconds. I knew he wasn't going to hire me anyway, and I had nothing to lose by being forthright. He stood up and extended his hand. "Well, Ethan, thanks for coming in."

Three weeks later I received a voicemail message from the interviewer actually offering me the position. Unfortunately, by the time I received it, I had completely forgotten about the job.

For my interview at Old Navy, I was placed at the end of a long table in a dimly lit basement room amidst cardboard boxes and fake plastic trees left over from the holiday season. Alongside me were seven or eight teenage girls and a guy who resembled a young, lanky John Lennon. The woman conducting the interview called it a "fun, relaxed group meeting." I assumed that, like a reality show, we would be kicked off one by one until they found that *one* special person who was truly worthy enough to sell their crappy clothing. She went around the table and asked us to stand, say our name, and tell the group a little bit about ourselves—I've never been to an AA meeting before, but I imagine this is what one feels like:

"Hello, I'm Ethan Reid."

"Hi, Ethan!" they all said.

"And I want to work at Old Navy because I'm broke and everybody thinks I'm a failure."

The interviewer piped in. "Well, no one *here* thinks that. Right, everybody?"

They all nodded in unison.

"Thanks, guys." I sat down.

For the next challenge, the interviewer passed a hat around the room containing little pieces of paper with questions written on them. John Lennon was the first to go: he unraveled his paper and read aloud, " 'Describe a time in which you went above and beyond the call of duty for someone.' " He rose from his chair and in a nasally voice answered: "Well, I remember this one time my sister had a really big math exam. We were sitting at the kitchen table and she was just *freaking out* because she didn't have a calculator to bring with her. So I calmly said, 'Look. Don't worry. We'll get through this somehow.' And then, I went upstairs, and I looked inside my desk and, lo and behold, there was a calculator. And so, I let her borrow that calculator . . ."

When he finished telling his story, the interviewer nodded and smiled and there was a long moment of silence before I inadvertently burst out laughing. Then the girls joined in. Even the interviewer was grinning. But I laughed harder than anyone else. Then I slammed my fist down on the table and pointed at Lennon and shouted, "Hire him! He wins!"

After the giggling subsided, I withdrew into my chair, still snickering and covering my mouth with the palm of my hand. The interviewer passed the hat onto me and said, "Your turn, Ethan."

"Alright," I said. "But I don't think I can top that calculator shit."

My ball of paper revealed the question, *Describe your greatest fear.* I stood up and read it aloud and then thought about my answer.

"My greatest fear . . . is *not* getting this job."

I nodded my head and grinned, pleased with myself for being so clever. And then I added, "Oh, and snakes."

I was eliminated from the first round and never heard from Old Navy again.

Six

Doc, Craig, Scott and I are huddled around the kitchen table playing a drinking game called Pyramid. Fifteen cards are placed face down on the table and arranged in a triangle with five cards at the bottom and one card at the top. Cards are then flipped over one by one as you work your way up the pyramid. Each level is worth more than the last, starting at one drink and ending with five. Once a card has been flipped, you can order someone to take a drink—assuming you have that same card in your hand. Bluffing also comes into play—you can order someone to take a drink even if you *don't* have the card. It's risky, though, because they can call your bluff, and whoever is in the wrong has to drink double the original amount. In short, Pyramid can get you hammered pretty quickly.

But you know how to drive, baby you're my ride blares from the stereo in the background, and a mix of marijuana and cigarette smoke lingers in the air. Scott flips over a jack on the fourth level of the pyramid; I don't have a jack, but I've been losing badly and so I try to bluff. "Craig! Take four drinks."

"Bullshit!" he says. "Show me!"

"Fuck!" I shout. The other guys laugh as they watch me grudgingly swallow eight mouthfuls of gin-and-tonic. I flip over the next card and it's a queen. Again, I don't have one.

"Reid! Drink!" says Scott.

"No way. Bluff. Let me see it."

He wades through his hand and then carefully plucks out a card with his thumb and forefinger and I already know by the expression on his face that it's a queen. "Goddammit!" I yell. Again, the table erupts into laughter as I'm forced to take another eight drinks. Having emptied my glass, I get up from the table and grab the ice cube tray from the freezer and make myself another. "Just turn over the last card. I won't have it anyway."

The top of the pyramid. This card is worth five drinks—ten if you're caught on a bluff. Scott flips it over to reveal an eight of hearts. Without an eight in my hand, I throw down my cards in disgust. Meanwhile, Doc and Craig start eying one another, each waiting for the other person to speak.

"Drink five times, Doc," Craig says ominously.

"No, *you* drink five times," Doc retorts.

"Bluff. I don't think you have it."

"Well, you don't have it either. I'll bet my goddamned life on it." Now they're staring eye to eye. Both players have called a bluff. The stakes are high. The tension is palpable. This is the most exciting thing that's happened all night.

Craig lays his hand down on the table and calmly turns over the last card. Eight of spades. Doc looks at it in shock and then starts laughing.

"You son of a bitch!"

"You don't have it?" Craig asks.

"No!"

"So you're wrong on two bluffs!"

"That means you've gotta drink *twenty* times."

"Fuck me!" Doc yells, knocking his cards off the table with one sweep of his arm. Then the three of us watch in awe as he arduously chokes down an entire glass of Jameson Irish Whiskey. Finally, red-faced and out of breath, he victoriously slams the empty glass onto the table. We applaud his effort but he remains silent, still staring at the empty glass in front of him. Then, without a word, he slowly rises from his chair, wipes his mouth and nonchalantly walks into the bathroom, closing the door quietly behind him while the rest of us snicker and cheer and high-five one another.

"You think he's okay in there?" Scott asks. As usual, he speaks with a listless, uninflected tone, yet seems genuinely concerned.

"Yeah, he's fine," says Craig. "I've never seen him get sick."

"Even after chugging vodka," I add, referring to a time in which we walked home from a house party and Doc brandished a bottle of Smirnoff and demanded we drink it right then and there. We passed the bottle around in a circle and drank it down until there was about a third left. Then Doc took off his shirt— why, we still don't know—and chugged the remainder while flexing his arms and cackling maniacally. The vodka was trickling down his chin. I'd never seen anything like it. The man can definitely hold his liquor.

Doc is a binge drinker. All of my friends are—Craig, Scott, everybody I know, even the girls. However, unlike me, they don't seem to suffer any of the adverse effects. It doesn't affect their memory, their appetite, their circadian rhythms, it doesn't prevent them from waking up in the morning or getting to work on time and they certainly don't need it every day. I suppose I just take it a step further than they do.

Still, they all drink excessively on the weekends, and for me, the weekends can't come soon enough. Sure, I don't mind drinking alone, but it's far better with friends, and these guys, no matter how sophomoric, are great company. Like me, they're perpetually single, so none of them have any delusions of landing a wife or a white picket fence anytime in the near future, and that gives us the freedom to do whatever we want, whenever we want. There are no responsibilities, commitments or constraints. Really, why would anybody settle down at such a young age? How exciting is it to stay at home on a Friday night? I've never understood why some people are so eager to grow old.

So instead, every weekend, we pool cash for a cab to take us to an overcrowded bar where we pay for overpriced drinks and then flirt and dance and jump around like idiots, but really, what's the alternative? It's better than spending a night alone in your apartment. Anything is better than that.

A minute later, Doc opens the door and is noticeably more disheveled than before. He returns to the table and collapses into his chair.

"Aren't you glad you came back?" I ask jokingly.

Scott is confused. "Doc was gone somewhere?"

"Yeah, Vancouver. He went to see his sister."

"Which one?" Craig asks. "The hot one?"

"*Nooo,*" Doc moans.

"Yup. She just had a kid."

"I wanna see his sister," says Scott, rising from his chair. The three of us saunter over to the computer while Doc rests his head sideways on the tabletop; he tries to object, but can only muster an incoherent groan. Craig logs onto Facebook and immediately finds a picture of Kelly standing on a sunny beach with her arm wrapped around the waist of another girl. Both are tanned and wearing brightly-coloured bikinis. Scott is impressed. "Wow. She *is* hot. She reminds me of my friend, Doug."

The three of us pause and look at one another.

"... Because he *also* has a hot sister," he adds.

Craig returns to the table and asks, "Who's this husband of hers anyway?"

"He's an alright guy," Doc says, rearing his head. "But he's German so, you know, he's got a lot to atone for. He's a massage therapist."

"Did he go to school for that?"

"Must've. You can't just start massaging people. But yeah, me and him went to this party, and he's German, so he was drinking all efficiently and shit, but I went overboard and ended up puking on the patio. The next morning I was so hungover I tried to clean it up with a rock."

Craig furrows his brow in disbelief. "*You* threw up? I've *never* seen you throw up. You have, like, an iron stomach."

"Iron? Come on. My stomach's harder than *that.*"

"Like what? Diamond?"

"No. Harder."

"Nothing's harder than diamond."

Doc thinks for a moment. "What about boron?"

"Boron?"

"Yeah!"

Craig scoffs. "Boron's not hard."

"Boron's *tough*, baby!" Doc yells.

Doc and Craig will fight about anything, but this is the first time I've heard them argue about the Periodic Table. I think that's the sign of a good friendship: when you can yell and scream at each other without getting angry. Both are well-read and opinionated, but they live at opposite ends of the political spectrum: Doc is an anti-government libertarian with a "screw-any-body-who-isn't-me" philosophy, whereas Craig is more compassionate and perhaps too idealistic, the kind of person who gets upset about the starving children in Africa but doesn't give a damn about people going hungry in his own backyard. Politically speaking, I suppose I fall somewhere in the middle. I can relate to Doc's apathy and indifference toward others—although I hate to admit it—but I used to be a lot more like

Craig. I think your idealism gradually fades as you get older. Cynicism is easier to believe in.

They continue to argue and bicker about boron for several minutes while Scott and I drink our gin-and-tonics on the couch. When their debate finally dies down, I calmly ask, "So, where are we going tonight?"

"A bar called the Phoenix," says Craig. "There's a band playing that's worth checking out."

Scott is puzzled. "Didn't you see it on Facebook?"

"Reid doesn't have Facebook."

"Why not?"

" 'Cause he's a weirdo."

"Man, you gotta get on Facebook."

Whenever I tell people I don't use social media, I get one of two reactions: what Scott just said, or *Good, don't get it, it'll take up all your time.* Either way, they always look at me like I'm an alien—or the last person on earth who hasn't joined their little club. To me, the whole concept seems entirely unnecessary. What's wrong with a phone call? Or an email? Or actually meeting someone face to face? It wasn't so long ago that everybody was telling me to get a Myspace page. Now it's Facebook. Soon it'll be something else. Where does it end?

The most egregious aspect of social media, in my opinion, is the fact that anything you post could potentially stay on the internet forever. People save it and pass it along. I say and do so many stupid things I would never want to be permanent. I don't want to leave a trace of myself anywhere. I'd rather be a ghost. Scorch the earth, that's my policy. And to be honest, I have no interest in seeing pictures of people I knew however many years ago. I prefer to keep my head in the sand. Regardless, this is an argument with society I'll never win, so I always lie and say, "I'll get on it eventually."

"Well, we should get going," Doc announces. We all look at the clock and nod in tacit agreement before swilling the rest of our drinks. Then we put on our shoes and turn off the lights and head downstairs to the city below.

SEVEN

At night, I come alive. In the daytime I feel like a fraud, a pariah hiding in plain sight. But when the sun sets and the streets go dark, that's the only time I feel truly at ease. My eyes are bright, my mind is alert, and my complexion, which is often red and blemished due to immoderation, is concealed beneath a veil of dim, artificial light. I never feel alone because there's always somebody willing to talk. Alcohol breaks down the walls, the barriers enforced by reticence and inhibition. People become more interesting to me and I approach them effortlessly. Normally, I withdraw from the world. At night, I become a different person. I embrace it.

The four of us wander down the centre of the road on our way to the Phoenix, each sporting a different style: Doc has short, sandy blonde hair and wears a red plaid shirt, unchanged from this morning; Craig has glasses and a striped green top featuring the logo of a band I've never heard of; and Scott is wearing a good old-fashioned Cosby sweater. In terms of presentability, I rank somewhere in the middle: my straight brown hair is slightly tousled and parted to the side and I'm wearing a blue dress shirt, a thin leather jacket and grey jeans. We each brought a can of beer with us, and anytime a police car drives by we conspicuously hide them underneath our shirts.

"I'm gonna text Amber!" Doc suddenly proclaims before drop-kicking his empty can into a nearby yard and spooking a cat. Amber is a girl we know from school that Doc has been sleeping with periodically for months. He speaks aloud as he types a text message on his phone, accentuating every word: "Dear. Baby. Can't. Wait. To. Get. All. Up. In. That. Ass. Love. Jeff." We all laugh and demand that he send it. He does.

When we arrive at the Phoenix, there's a short lineup of people stretching from the sidewalk to the front door where two bouncers are checking IDs. Once we're inside we pay the cover and walk through a narrow, L-shaped hallway. The red walls are adorned with black-and-white photographs of musical acts that have played the stage, but it's too dark to read any of the names.

The hallway leads us into the main venue: a massive room the size of a high school gymnasium with bars on either side and a giant stage to our right. Opposite the stage is a balcony equipped with its own bar and several black leather couches. We buy our drinks upstairs and then commandeer two couches and a long table. I ask Scott what band we're seeing tonight, but the music is too loud for me to hear his answer, so I lean forward and ask him again.

"Silverchest!" he repeats.

"Who the hell is that?"

"Man, you've never heard of Silverchest?" Craig says as he takes a seat beside me. "They're amazing."

"Yeah?"

"I downloaded their first album last night," says Scott. "It's awesome. You'll like them.".

"Ah, I dunno. I don't really listen to a lot of new stuff."

"Why not?"

"I just got tired of it. I think we ran out of ideas. It's all recycled and auto-tuned now. We can't play any faster, or scream any harder, or write any songs better than what they did in the sixties, so what's the point? Somewhere around that last Woodstock, when those assholes were setting everything on fire, we should have just given up. Waved the white flag."

Scott considers what I've said before adding, "Woodstock '99 was *definitely* one of the best Woodstocks of all time."

"Oh yeah," I deadpan. "Definitely in the top five."

"You've gotta look harder, man," says Craig. "There's lots of good music being made nowadays. Nobody cares about the videos anymore, so your image doesn't matter, and new bands can post all their stuff online, so radio stations and record labels aren't really necessary either. There are no rules. It's the way it should be. You're just being a dick."

I like Craig, but he's somewhat of a hipster and often exhibits many of their holier-than-thou personality traits. Hipsters claim to be devoted music fans, but at the same time they disapprove of anything that's popular, so in reality it's not about the actual *songs* for them—if it were, a band's popularity would be completely irrelevant. They're also very fickle; quick to anoint an up-and-coming band as the next Nirvana and just as quick to dismiss said band for having "sold-out" because they made enough money to buy a van and tour Wisconsin. The truth is: hipsters want that feeling of superiority that comes along with being one of the few people who know about a particular artist or band. Once that's gone, they go looking for the next indie act to latch onto. Weird music is preferable to good music and they often can't make the distinction. They're also unnecessarily opinionated about things that *do not matter* and abruptly piss on anything that doesn't meet their ridiculously high standards. Nothing makes a hipster happier than playing the devil's advocate, which gives them an opportunity to display their pretentious, faux-intellectual prowess. They're a drag. They're socially awkward and a pain to be around. And they can't drink worth shit. I've met jocks, nerds, gamers, goths, punkrockers and metalheads, and I would take any of them any day of the week over a hipster.

Fortunately, Craig isn't nearly as bad as the rest of them. And he can drink. Nonetheless, when it comes to music, he definitely has that hipster mentality. I can't really fault him, though; he works at a music store and is therefore constantly surrounded by hipsters. One time, he told me his dream was to form a band that sounds like Dinosaur Jr. meets The Strokes, but he can't seem to find any like-minded individuals who share his vision—probably because everybody he meets is a goddamn hipster.

"I don't know," I mutter, "I just haven't heard any new bands that are any good. I mean, nothing affects me the way *In Utero* or *Siamese Dream* or *OK Computer* did the first time I heard them."

"Don't worry," Scott says. "Silverchest will change all that."

I notice Doc hasn't said a word in several minutes, and this is the kind of discussion he usually revels in. He loves talking about old punk rock records from bands like The Adolescents, Bad Brains, Jawbreaker and Operation Ivy and then explaining in great detail how and why the genre has been in decline since the late eighties. Instead, he's staring down at his phone, typing text messages with an uneasy expression on his face. When we ask him what's wrong, he tells us a girl he recently slept with just informed him that she may have contracted a sexually transmitted disease from an ex-boyfriend.

"Ah, you'll be fine," I assure him.

"You wore a condom, right?" Craig asks.

"God no!" he says with a disgusted look on his face. "Never! Everybody knows that. I play the skins!"

We gradually dissolve into laughter.

Doc takes umbrage. "It's not funny!"

"It's kinda funny," says Craig.

"You have crabs now," Scott deadpans.

Doc lowers his head and nervously fiddles with his thumbs. "Actually she says it might be chlamydia."

We start laughing again and Doc angrily stands up from the couch.

"C'mon, we're joking!" I say. "Where are you going?"

"To the bathroom. I gotta go check my balls."

We sneer and chuckle as he hurries downstairs.

"Shit, I don't know what he's so worried about," says Craig. "You go to a doctor, get some antibiotics, and you can bust that shit out in a week."

Ten minutes later, I go to the bathroom in search of Doc but the stalls are empty and there's no sign of him anywhere. I relieve myself and then wash my hands and walk back into the crowd only to find the lights have dimmed as the band is about to take the stage. The guitarist is illuminated by a single beam of light and he's picking one string at a time in a crescendo of notes that rise, echo, and fall. Then the bassist is introduced. I look around at the audience and even in the darkness I can see the elation on their faces: they're staring at the stage with widened eyes, gape-mouthed like fish, completely in awe.

Suddenly the drummer smashes his sticks against the cymbals as the lights flare and the audience erupts into applause as the singer is finally revealed: a skinny woman in her mid-forties with straggly blonde hair and a silver washboard hanging from her neck. She moves up to the microphone and taps the metal with her fingertips to produce a dull, repetitive sound.

"YEAH! SILVERCHEST!" a fat man screams from behind me, pumping his balled fist into the air. I leer at the band and listen with contempt as they play slow, boring experimental music. After the first song, the singer retrieves a trash can from behind the drum kit and sporadically hits it with a large wooden stick. I scan the crowd and the people are going absolutely bananas. They love it. The third song they play is called "Your Golden Soul" and it's even worse than the first two. Disinterested, I stand at the bar for the rest of their set, drinking shots of whiskey by myself with my back facing the stage.

EIGHT

The concert mercifully ends and the crowd begins to shuffle through the hallway and out onto the street. I've lost track of my friends and so I wait for them on the sidewalk by the entrance. A homeless man with tattoos, a shaved head and a loose black sweater—he can't be much older than I am—approaches from the road and asks me for spare change. Says he wants to buy a coffee.

"Yeah, sure man," I reply, reaching into my back pocket. I find a few coins and count them in the palm of my hand. Three dollars. "Sorry I don't have more for ya."

He takes the money from me and says, incredulously, "Aw, c'mon, you gotta have more than that. Check your wallet."

I'm slightly taken aback by the imposition. "I don't keep change in my wallet. Besides, I thought three dollars was pretty good."

"Nah, man, you gotta have more."

"I thought you just wanted a coffee?"

"Coffee's expensive these days."

"What kind are you buying? A fucking latte macchiato?" I've learned a few things about coffee since my failed job interview.

"Come on, man!" he demands. "You've got more!"

"No! In fact, I want my three bucks back."

"You serious?"

"If you're gonna be like that, I want it back."

"No way! Fuck you!" he shouts before sprinting off down the middle of the road. My three friends arrive just in time to see him go.

"What the hell was that about?" Doc asks.

"Panhandler! Didn't like my three bucks!"

"Weird."

"Why do homeless guys always wanna buy a coffee anyway? Why not get something more filling, like a can of Chef Boyardee?"

"His ravioli is delicious," says Scott.

"Exactly!"

"Man, don't even worry about it," Doc assures me. "The guy must be crazy. He's probably pissing and shitting himself right now. Probably has shit running down his leg."

"Maybe you're right."

"Craig here wants to go to a bar in Cabbagetown. It's kinda small, but the music is good. They play a lot of, uh . . ." Doc snaps his fingers while trying to recall a name. "Who's that gay guy that plays piano?"

"Rufus Wainwright?"

"No, the other one."

"Elton John?"

"Bingo!"

The walk to Parliament Street is relatively short and I'm surprised at how small the pub is once we arrive. Half of the clientele is smoking cigarettes on the front deck and the other half is standing shoulder-to-shoulder in the narrow space between the bar and the dining area. The decor is very casual, like the living room of an old Victorian home, with green carpets, a fireplace and dark wooden furniture. We manage to seize the one empty table in the corner by the window, and while Craig is off at the bar ordering our drinks one of the waitresses stops and squints and puts her hand on my shoulder.

"Hey! I remember you. It's Ethan, right?"

I haven't the faintest idea who she is, but I feign recognition anyway, as I always do. "Yeah! Hey! How's it going?"

"Good! Haven't seen you in a while. What you been up to?"

"Uh . . . you might have me confused with somebody else, actually. This is my first time here."

"No I've seen you here before. What, you don't remember? You sat right over *there*." She points to a stool on the other side of the bar. "I remember because you ate a bunch of chili peppers and then drank straight vinegar."

"That doesn't sound like me."

"Trust me. It was you."

"Why would I do that?"

"To impress the girl sitting next to you."

"Really? Did it work?"

"No!" she scoffs, then laughs and walks away.

Maybe I have been here before. Though I doubt I would ever drink vinegar to impress a girl, no matter how drunk I was. I hate vinegar. And how is that impressive? Still, she seemed fairly adamant.

While I'm pondering it, I notice Craig calling me over to the bar to help him carry some drinks back to the table. I meet him at the counter and he leans into my ear and whispers, "Man, you gotta talk to this guy" while gesturing to the old fellow sitting next to him dressed from head to toe in grey fisherman attire. He has a raincoat, a bucket hat, a prickly grey beard, an eyepatch, and he's missing several teeth. He looks like the kind of guy you would expect to find on a box of fish sticks. In his right hand he holds two metal spoons and he clinks them together against his thigh. "Meet my friend, Ethan," Craig tells him before quietly making his escape.

"Hello, Spoonman," I say, shaking his hand. He responds to me in gibberish; I can't make out any of the words, but he's smiling and laughing and so I smile too. Then he looks down at the spoons and starts to play a beat. It has no discernible melody.

"Hey, do you know 'Hey Jude'?" I ask him.

He grits his teeth and makes a loud, guttural noise, which I assume to mean, "Yes." Then, with quick, erratic movements, he jingles the spoons in such a way that sounds absolutely nothing like "Hey Jude." I sing a few of the lyrics anyway.

"Hey, how about I play a song with you?" I say. "We'll have a jam session." I flag down the bartender and ask her for a pair of spoons.

"I'm sorry," she tells me, "but we don't give out spoons at night anymore."

"Why not?"

She lowers her head and whispers, "Well, unfortunately, some people were taking them into the bathroom and using them to light up heroin. All of our spoons kept going missing."

"Really?" I say, motioning to Spoonman. "Are you sure *this guy* didn't steal them all?" Spoonman bellows out in disapproval and then laughs. Heartily. He reminds me of one of those walking trees from *The Lord of the Rings*.

"Yeah, I'm sure," she says. "We caught them in there a couple of times. It was sad. And now we keep the spoons on lockdown."

"Okay. Thanks anyway." I turn back to the fisherman and we shake hands again. "Well, it's been a hell of a ride, Spoonman." He pats me on the arm and then mumbles something that sounds like "Goodbye, friend." I grab the scotch Craig ordered me and clink it against his pint of cider and then return to the table. I notice Doc is missing.

"He went outside to make a phone call," Craig tells me. And then, right on cue, Doc rushes back into the bar and impatiently pushes through the crowd to huddle beside us.

"Okay, we're on," he says emphatically.

"What's on?" I ask.

"Amber and her friends are at Panorama. We've gotta drink up and go."

"C'mon, man," I object. "We just got here. Let's stick around for at least a drink or two."

"Nah, we gotta go now. Trust me. It'll be fun. Natalie's there too."

Natalie. I'm crazy about Natalie. I met her late last year when she was playing a show with her indie pop band *The Crunchy Mondays*—that name always makes me laugh. She's absolutely beautiful: she has long dark hair with red highlights, striking eyes, and her smile—the one she makes when she finds something really, really funny—just kills me. Thankfully, I can make her laugh pretty often. Whenever our mutual friends meet up at a bar, we usually spend the entire night talking and ignoring everybody else. She's the first girl I've had any real hope for since Rachael.

Unfortunately, Natalie lives in the suburbs and works two part-time jobs, so she's a hard person to get a hold of. The chemistry is definitely there between us, but when we're not in the same room she seems completely indifferent to me, like I'm an afterthought. I occasionally give her a call and ask about her plans for the weekend, but the correspondence is always one-way. In fact, I haven't seen her in over a month. As far as I know, she doesn't have a boyfriend—she tells everyone she's too busy for a relationship—but still, I can't make sense of it. Maybe that's why I'm so infatuated: she's unpredictable, mysterious, and impossible to comprehend.

A few months ago, a large group of us went to an animal shelter to look at the puppies. Nobody had any intention of adopting one—we just wanted to gawk at them because they're cute. The dogs barked and pawed at us from behind thin metal bars, crying out with open mouths and round eyes, and it was difficult not to take one home. While most tried to get our attention, there was this one dog that simply lay down in the middle of his cage and stared at me. I put my hand up to the bars and he gently licked my fingers. He was brown, with white patches and dark circles around his eyes, and his fur was a bit straggly. It seemed as if he was nursing an old injury. I wanted to take him with us. Natalie urged me to buy him. For a moment I wondered what it would be like to live an ordinary life in the suburbs with her and the dog and a boring job and it actually didn't seem so bad—but I knew that was just a pipe dream.

"What would you call him?" she asked me.

"Interceptor," I deadpanned.

She laughed. Said it was a funny name for a dog.

"Okay, yeah, we should probably check this out," I tell the guys.

Doc grins and slaps the table. "Cool! You guys coming?"

"Yeah, sure," says Scott, his speech beginning to slur. "But I wanna get laid tonight. It's been awhile. And I wanna buy some weed."

"Didn't you hook up with a girl last weekend?" Craig asks. "At that birthday party?"

"Nah, we didn't do anything."

"What happened?"

"Well, I was really into this girl and she was pretty attractive and I told her I hadn't had sex in, like, three months, and she said, 'Try two years!' So I was flirting with her pretty hard and she was giving me the eyes and then Doug started eating a jar of mayo and I got distracted. And then I just, y'know, kinda wandered off."

A brief moment of silence ensues before Craig explodes into laughter. "That's it? You were busy watching a guy eat *mayo*?"

"It was a big jar."

"I don't know why," Doc interjects, "but Amber sounded kinda pissed off at me. I might not be getting laid tonight, but goddammit, I'm gonna try."

"You have chlamydia!" Craig reminds him.

"That remains to be seen. Besides, I can still spoon her."

NINE

In the cab, I'm crammed between Doc and Craig in the middle of the backseat. Our cab driver is a balding, middle-aged man in an old brown jacket. He has no neck, only shoulders, and he speaks with a Middle Eastern accent. When I'm drunk I have no qualms about initiating conversation with anyone, so after we state our destination I immediately ask the driver, "How's your night going?"

"Ah, I'm not too happy about it."

"Why's that?"

"It's slow, man! Business is very slow, much slower than it used to be, you know? It's the recession. I think the reason is, people have less money, so they go out less. It affects the business. I mean, I thank God I still have a job and I haven't been laid off yet, so I can still put food on the table and feed my family, but it should be better. . . . It should be better than this."

His words seem to hang in the air. I reflect on what he's said, what he's going through, and I empathize. I can't imagine how difficult it must be to be a parent, to have to provide for others, to know you're solely responsible for their well-being and their security and whether or not they eat dinner that night. And the fear that must come when you realize you might be unable to take care of them due to reasons beyond your control—because of governments or economic fluctuations or the price of gas. A long, lingering silence envelops us. And then Scott asks, "Do you have any weed?"

The driver laughs. "No! I can't spend money on that kind of thing. I have to buy shoes for my kids. They'll be back in school pretty soon . . . and there's always something they need. Can't be spending money on things like that."

"Hmm. We have different priorities, I guess."

The taxi stops at Bay and Bloor where tall office buildings and high-end stores surround us in all directions. I tip the driver well and thank him for the ride and then follow the guys into an empty shopping mall. At the far end we enter a black elevator and push a button for the fifty-first floor. Nobody says a word, except for Scott, who mumbles to himself, "I hope I get laid tonight." It's past midnight and we're all intoxicated, but I still feel anxious; Natalie is on the other side of these doors and I'm always apprehensive when I'm about to see her.

The elevator opens and we're immediately greeted by a formally dressed maître d' who ushers us to a table. The restaurant gets its name from the one-hundred-and-eighty degree view of downtown Toronto; you can see the entire skyline via the large glass windows and adjoining balcony that surrounds the room. Surprisingly, the place isn't busy—I suppose the type of people who frequent fancy cocktail bars don't often stay out past midnight. Then, through the window, I catch a glimpse of Natalie standing alone outside smoking a cigarette with her back to me. Behind her, the city shines brightly in a cascade of red, blue and purple. Without saying a word, I leave the others and open the glass door to the balcony, and she glances over her shoulder and spots me just as I arrive.

"Ethan!" she says, smiling and wrapping her arms around me. She's wearing the usual perfume and it smells like shea. I read somewhere that being at a higher elevation increases our feelings of attraction; it might have something to do with the thinner air or the adrenaline rush induced by our fear of heights, but either way, I believe it. "I heard you might show up."

"Yeah, we just got here. How's it going?"

"Awesome! I'm glad you came. Wanna smoke?" She pulls a cigarette from her pack and I light it by pressing it against the one in her mouth.

"So, how's your summer been? I haven't seen you in a while."

"Oh it's been crazy," she says. "I've been super busy with the band and everything. Tonight we played a show down at this club on Spadina."

"How'd it go?"

"It was good! Decent crowd. And we didn't screw up too much. I think we're getting better."

"Cool. I've gotta see you guys play again sometime." I haven't seen them do a live show since the first time we met. They were kind of sloppy, to be honest, but I hardly noticed; Natalie made up for any mistakes with her bouncy self-confidence and stage presence, so the imperfections of the band didn't matter. Besides, the songs were catchy—I still have one stuck in my head.

"You should! We sound way better now. We've been practic-ing, like, two or three times a week. What about you? What've you been up to?"

Drinking. Smoking. Popping pills. "Not much, really," I say. "Just trying to find a new job since I quit the call centre. And I'm still waiting to hear back from the law schools I applied to."

Months ago, when I was having an internal crisis about my life and future, I decided to write the Law School Admission Test on a snowy day in February. The exam was five hours long and it tested logical reasoning and reading comprehension skills. I scored fairly high—not well enough to be accepted into any school of my choosing, but, with a good application letter, I certainly had a chance. And while I wasn't dead set on becoming a lawyer, I figured applying to law school would, at the very least, impress people. Better than telling them I was unemployed, anyway.

"Really? Where'd you apply?"

"Just the ones around Ontario, like Windsor, Queens, Osgoode Hall. . . . But yeah, I haven't heard anything back yet."

"That's cool. I never had you pegged as a lawyer though," she says coyly.

"Yeah, me neither. Gotta grow up sometime, right?" I pause before adding, "Anyway, can I get you a drink or something?"

"I'm good, thanks. Somebody left their water here." She holds up a glass of ice water and dangles it in front of her face. "I might drink this. Think it'll be okay? It doesn't look like they touched it," she adds, inspecting the rim.

"There could be germs."

"Yeah. Probably syphilis."

"Let me try it." She hands me the glass and I take a sip. "Hmm. Tastes like syphilis."

"I knew it!"

"You have to try it too. I don't wanna be the only one here with syphilis."

She laughs and takes a drink. "Ew! It burns!"

Natalie and I spend the next few minutes catching up, talking about the people we know, the places she's visited over the summer, and whatever else was new. When she speaks, I can't focus on anything else and time passes quickly. She can turn any mundane, trivial activity into an interesting story with her natural enthusiasm and that ever-changing expression on her face. Everything seems better when she's around, so when she tells me she has to leave because she's driving her brother to the airport in the morning, it completely takes the wind out of my sails.

"We should get together soon though!" she says.

"Yes! We should. I have so many great, great anecdotes to share with you," I say with a hint of sarcasm.

She smiles. "I'm sure you do."

"What about tomorrow night? I don't have any plans yet."

"Maybe. I've gotta work in the afternoon, but maybe after that? How about you give me a call and we'll set something up, okay?"

"Sounds good."

She hugs me again and I wish her goodnight and then she disappears. Still in a daze, I stare out at the city and it looks peaceful and silent, like it did this morning. Even though I was happy to see her, I can't help but feel despondent now that she's gone. I replay the entire exchange in my mind, trying to interpret the signals, wondering if she actually has any interest in me: she stood close, she played with her hair, her body language was open, but she was also quick to leave and noncommittal for tomorrow night. I wish I knew what she was thinking.

Resting my arms against the railing, breathing in and out, I glance down at my feet and then back at the city again. Then I notice Doc and Amber sitting across from each other at the other end of the balcony and I unintentionally eavesdrop on their conversation. Her voice is low and agitated:

"He saw your text messages, Jeffrey. Now he's worried there's something going on between us and he's all angry because he thinks I lied to him."

"Well, you *did* kinda lie to him."

"No I didn't!"

"Why don't you just tell him what's up?"

"I can't. Not now. We have a good thing going."

"No, *we* have a good thing going. He sucks."

"I'm sorry, Jeff. Why'd you have to send me those texts?"

"I didn't think he'd go through your phone! What's wrong with this guy? He's paranoid. I bet he's got a bunch of STDs too."

"*What?* Anyway, I'm sorry, but we can't keep doing this. And you can't keep texting me at, like, two in the morning. My phone vibrates and Justin's there and it's really awkward. I don't like it."

"Look," he whispers, "why don't we just go back to your place and spoon? Then we can talk about this in the morning."

Pause.

"As great as that sounds, I'm gonna pass."

Amber begins to rise from her chair and Doc interrupts her by placing his hand on her wrist. "Wait, don't go yet. There's something else you should know. . . ."

"What?"

He inhales deeply and pauses, considering for a moment. Then he shakes his head. "Never mind."

Amber peers back at him with a dumbfounded expression and then gives him a brief hug before leaving through the balcony door. Doc sits and stares at the table for a few seconds, probably wondering where he went wrong, until he sees me watching in the background.

"Reid! Man, you hear any of that? Psh. Didn't go well!"

"Sure didn't."

"I was gonna tell her about the whole chlamydia thing, but then I thought, y'know, fuck it."

"I'm sure she'll find out eventually."

"Exactly!" Then he clasps his hands together and rubs them back and forth before asking, "So! Where's Natalie?"

"She had to go, but we're supposed do something tomorrow night. Hopefully."

"Cool. Well, fuck this shit. Let's go back inside."

The two of us leave the balcony and rejoin Craig and Scott, who have continued to drink heavily in our absence. There are several empty pint glasses on the table and Scott is noticeably less coordinated than before. With Natalie out of the picture I see no reason to stay at this bar any longer. "Well, I think I'm gonna call it a night. I wanna catch the subway before it stops."

"What?" Doc objects. "Why on God's green fuck would you do that? The night's still young!"

"It's very young," Craig mutters. "It's like . . . prepubescent."

"Yeah, but I'm still hungover, and I don't wanna take the late bus."

"Get Scott to drive you!" says Doc. "He left his car at my place."

"He can't drive. Look at him! Look at his stupid face!" I point at Scott from across the table and he feebly smiles back at me with vacant eyes.

"He's fine!"

"I'm alright," Scott mumbles. "I can drive . . . if you want."

"Really?" I say skeptically. Then I pull my keys from my pocket and shout, "Scott! Think fast!" before throwing them at his face. He doesn't catch them or even raise his hands to defend himself. He doesn't react. The metal keys hit him squarely between the eyes and make a loud *ping* sound as they knock his head back. Doc and Craig start laughing.

"Ow," he yelps.

"See?" I say, picking up my keys. "I'm taking the subway."

"What's going on tomorrow night?" Craig asks.

"I don't know yet. We'll figure it out."

"Alright, cool man. Take it easy."

I wave goodbye to the group and take the elevator down to the ground floor and then exit through the empty mall. Once outside, I cross a quiet intersection, and when I arrive at the subway station the last train of the night is waiting to take me north. There are no other people on the platform and the train feels empty. Everything is silent. As the train passes through a dark tunnel, I stare at my reflection in the window and the edge of the glass distorts my face so that my cheekbone seems to sag, my jawline looks ghoulish and unnaturally thin, and my eye appears to be nothing more than a hollow, blackened pit.

TEN

As I get off the train at Eglinton Station the sharp pain in my chest suddenly returns and I lose my breath. It often hits me at night: a crippling tightness in my heart that makes it difficult to inhale. I know I'll need another drink if I'm to fall asleep—a night cap, a libation, whatever you want to call it, I need it. I exit the station and hunch forward while clutching the left side of my chest for a block or two until I pass by another cocktail bar called Coquine. Inside, people are still standing and drinking beneath the neon blue lighting—an older crowd, mostly, well-dressed in suits and ties and expensive outfits. I cut through the flock and eventually find an empty stool at the end of the silver bar. The bartender pours me a double scotch on the rocks and I sip it and the pain gradually subsides. I quietly keep to myself, watching sport highlights on the television in the corner and staring at the various bottles of colourful liqueurs that adorn the shelf.

Later, as I'm trying to find the washroom, I come across a small table where a woman is holding a camera and taking a picture of what I can only assume are her two friends: one male and one female. She appears to be in her early thirties and she has curly brown hair and a low-cut black dress revealing ample cleavage. Sensing an opportunity to help her out—and to strike up a conversation—I fearlessly approach.

"Hey, I can take a picture of the three of you if you want."

"Oh, no, that's okay," she says.

"Really, it's no problem."

She leans into my ear and whispers, "I don't want to be in any pictures tonight."

"Why not? You look great."

"Because I'm cheating on my husband right now."

I try to remain composed, act unsurprised, but I'm sure she can tell by my inadvertently raised eyebrows that I'm somewhat taken aback. "Well, we've all been in *that* situation before."

"Not me. This is my first time."

"My name's Ethan."

"Melanie." She shakes my hand and her grip is soft. I don't know what else to say, so I simply offer her encouragement.

"Well I hope this whole affair thing works out for you."

"Yeah, me too."

"I just want you to be happy, Melanie," I say, touching her shoulder and tilting my head to the side in a gesture of sincerity. "I'll be at the bar if you need a drink."

About half an hour later I'm surprised to find Melanie pulling up a stool beside me. She orders a vodka martini and then shifts her body to face me. Fortunately, I'm significantly more intoxicated than I was before and brimming with self-confidence; I've even introduced myself to the bartender, Marty, who was kind enough to offer me a sample of Grey Goose on the house. "Customer appreciation," he called it.

"You can put her martini on my tab," I tell Marty. Then I look at her and ask, "What happened to your suitor?"

"He had to leave early."

"I see. I'm probably more interesting than him anyway."

I take a sip and she smiles. "What do you do, Ethan?"

I need to come up with something. Fast. Can't let her know I'm an out-of-work ne'er-do-well who doesn't contribute to society in any meaningful way. I'm currently enrolled in the journalism program at Ryerson, so I decide to run with it. "I'm a journalist."

"Really? What kind? Like, print?"

"Yeah. Freelance, mostly."

"Where have you been published?"

"Oh, y'know, the Star, the Globe and Mail, that paper they hand out for free on the subway. . . ." Desperately wanting to change the subject, I ask, "What about you?"

"I'm a teacher. Third grade. Up in North York. We're on our summer break right now."

"Cool. Do you like it?"

"It's great. I love it."

"What about the kids? They give you any trouble? If so, I can sort 'em out," I say, grinding my fist into my palm.

"Nah, we get along fine. Well, there's always one in every group. I'll show you." She opens her purse and pulls out a class picture—the kind we used to have before digital cameras were invented. It feels nice to hold an actual photo again.

"See this guy right here?" She points to a kid in the front row wearing a green sweater with red hair, freckles and a goofy smile on his face. "That's Kevin. He's a little cocksucker, that one."

"A cocksucker, huh?"

"Yeah. Huge prick. Huge! His parents are pricks too. He made my life a living hell the first month. He has A.D.D. and is probably obsessive-compulsive."

"So how'd you straighten him out?"

"Well, eventually we had a meeting and the doctor decided to put him on Ritalin. That definitely slowed him down.

Sometimes I just bribed him with candy," she says with a grin. "If he could be quiet for the whole day, I'd give him something sweet at the end. We got along great after that."

"One in every group," I repeat.

After a brief pause, she asks, "Do you smoke?" as she retrieves a pack of menthol cigarettes from her purse.

"Like a goddamn chimney! I go through two lighters a day."

She smiles, not realizing I stole that joke from Bill Hicks.

"Let's go outside."

After finishing her pack of menthols and ordering a few more drinks before last call, I ask Melanie if she wants to come back to my place, split a bottle of wine and see what happens. Soon we're standing in front of my apartment room door on the stained blue carpeting, and we're slurring and giggling and her body is leaning into mine with her arm wrapped tightly around my waist. My room is still a mess—an accomplished, upstanding journalist of my supposed reputation would never live in a dump like this—but I've come too far to back out now.

"Do you have any roommates?" she asks as I fiddle with the keys.

"Yeah. He's really messy. Just . . . disorganized. I think I'm gonna tell him to move out." As soon as we're through the door, she immediately pushes me up against the wall and starts kissing me, occasionally biting down on my lower lip. Her mouth tastes like an ashtray, but it still feels good. Then she stops for a moment to survey the room.

"Wow, he *is* messy."

We start kissing again, and with my eyes closed I lead her toward the bedroom while trying to avoid all of the clothes and garbage on the floor. "Yeah, messy guy. That's why I call him Tornado. He destroys everything in his path."

As I'm guiding her through the apartment, her foot catches on a pair of boxer briefs and she trips and falls to the hardwood floor. I expect her to wince in pain, but she just snorts and laughs it off. I help her upright and we continue the foreplay without missing a beat. Then I accidentally smash my knee on the metal leg of a table. "Fuck! My knee!"

Damaged and bruised, we finally make it onto the bed. I worry I might be too drunk to engage in any carnal activity, which is often the case, but thankfully I'm not entirely numb yet. As her clothes come off, I feel that air of accomplishment and validation every man feels anytime he adds another notch to his belt. But when I start to fuck her—a married woman—the feeling is diminished, followed swiftly by an overwhelming sense of guilt, sadness and self-loathing.

—Part ii—

Into the Nadir

The audience has been lied to. That's the first thought that flows through my mind as I wake. Lied to by books, television and movies, conditioned to believe that life and love can be explained in ninety minutes or less and that what happens here actually matters. It's all just smoke and mirrors. In the real world there is no studio audience, no third act resolution, no storybook ending. We were lied to again and again: by the sycophantic politicians who sold us out for campaign contributions; the advertisers who bombarded us with imagery designed to feed off our insecurities; the priests who told us to be kind to others while they were busy sodomizing children; the anti-drug campaigners who warned us that smoking marijuana would be fatal; the economists who predicted that globalization would lead us all to prosperity; and the school teachers who taught us to believe we could be anything we wanted to be. Liars. All of them.

I was too young to remember the fall of the Berlin Wall, but I know what it represented: an opportunity to remake the world, to get it right this time, with freedom, equality and justice for all. The Doomsday Clock was set at seventeen minutes to midnight. Seventeen! But we squandered that opportunity. In a few short years we became fat and complacent and let a small group of wealthy CEOs buy the politicians, ruin the planet and kill the middle class, and now they've pit us against each other to fight over the scraps. If you, like me, had any delusion that your existence on this earth would amount to more than just a hill of beans, imagine your dismay when you begin to realize you were wrong from the very start. The game is rigged. There are no goddamn beans. And we've all bought into the lie.

I'm lying naked on a mattress with my body only partially covered by a thin blue blanket. The balcony door is wide open and cold morning air is flowing into the room—I don't know why I opened it last night. My head aches and my throat is dry and I can only remember the evening in fragments. I'm not even sure if I paid my tab—they might still have my credit card at the cocktail bar. Melanie is nowhere to be found. Did she leave already? I hope she did. The last time I brought a girl home, she didn't leave until well into the afternoon. Just kept sleeping and snoring while I lay awake in bed staring at the ceiling. Eventually I had to wake her up and tell her I was going to be late for work. That was a lie. I went to the liquor store and bought a bottle of scotch and drank on my futon that day.

Suddenly I hear Melanie rustling in the bathroom, and a moment later she returns wearing the same black dress she wore the night before—albeit with her hair and make-up slightly askew. I squint my eyes, exhale, stretch out my arms and mumble, "Good morning." How many times have I awoken to an awkward situation like this? I've been doing it for years and I never get any better at it. Never know what to do or what to say.

"Hey what's with all the medication in your bathroom?" she asks. "Are you alright?"

She opened the medicine cabinet. Great. I should really get a padlock for that. "Yeah, I'm fine. I just . . . I have trouble sleeping sometimes."

"I see."

"Do you want some breakfast? I can make you bacon and eggs or something?"

"No, that's okay. I'm allergic to eggs anyway."

"Well, I probably have some Corn Flakes or Lucky Charms around here. . . . They've got those marshmallows and shit—"

"No, really, I'm fine. I should probably get going."

For some reason I don't want her to leave. Not yet. Not because I'm afraid I'll miss her, but because I feel like I've done something wrong. "At least let me buy you breakfast? There's a good place down the street from here."

She reluctantly accepts and I throw on some dirty clothes and we go.

It's ten o'clock in the morning and I'm sitting across from Melanie at a small table in a quiet diner. The radio in the background is barely audible over the sound of the wall clock and every tick of the second hand feels like an hour. Without alcohol, I realize, Melanie and I don't have anything in common and there's very little for us to talk about. I'm also unshaven, greasy-haired and probably smell like three different kinds of hard liquor.

Our food finally arrives and we start eating. She ordered pancakes, sausages and whole-wheat toast while I got a bowl of fruit and a glass of water because my stomach is too queasy to digest anything more substantial.

"How's the toast?" I ask her.

"It's good," she says, chewing quietly. "It's good toast."

"Hmm. That's good to hear."

A few awkward seconds pass. I take a loud sip of water between mouthfuls and then glance down at her left hand and notice she's not wearing her wedding ring. She takes another small bite of toast and says, "So, that roommate you mentioned . . . he doesn't exist, right?"

"Who? Tornado?"

"Yeah."

"No."

"So that was all your stuff? All the trash? The bottles?"

"Uh huh."

"I also noticed you had a class schedule on your fridge."

"Hmm. That's a pretty astute observation."

"You're still a student? You're not really a journalist?"

"No. Not yet, anyway. These days, it's kinda hard to, y'know, get your stuff out there and—"

"Are you always this full of shit?"

"Well . . ."

"And do you work? Or just drink all day?"

"I'm actually between jobs at the moment . . . but I do have somebody helping me with my résumé."

The waitress comes by to refill my water.

"Really? You can't eat any eggs?" I ask.

"No."

While chewing on a large piece of cantaloupe, I add, "You mean you've never had a *really* good omelette? With ham?"

"Oh God," she gasps, dropping her fork onto the plate and covering her face in embarrassment. She's obviously upset. It's understandable: she cheated on her husband with a drunken, unemployed loser ten years younger than she is.

"Look, I'm sorry," I say. "I don't even know what happened last night. Honestly, it seems like every day I wake up and I can't remember what I did the day before. It got so bad that, recently, I started writing everything down in a journal, just so I wouldn't forget. Basic things, y'know, like where I went, what I did, who I ran into, what we said to each other, where I—"

"Why are you telling me this?" she snaps.

I pause. "In a couple of days I probably won't remember you. At all. Your name, your face—it'll be like none of this ever happened."

Melanie remains quiet with her eyes focused on her plate, leisurely stirring her food around in a circle while I keep talking.

"You can still patch things up with whats-his-name. You're great. He's a lucky guy. I'm sure he knows that."

"I don't know what I'm gonna do," she sighs. Reaching into her purse, she retrieves a twenty-dollar bill and places it on the tablecloth as she rises from her chair. "It's on me. Good luck with the job hunt, Ethan."

Seconds later, Melanie leaves through the front door and I'm left staring at her empty chair. With a big chunk of melon in my mouth, I point at her plate with my fork and mumble, "Hey, you forgot your toast!"

TWELVE

It's around two o'clock in the afternoon and I'm still hungover. I don't even have the energy to shit, shower and shave. My bedroom is hot and sweltering with no air conditioning; there's nothing but a desk fan oscillating on the nightstand and the sunlight is seeping in through the blinds. Hungry, I throw on a pair of jeans and my blue dress shirt from last night and wander down the street to a pizza place on the corner. Inside, it's even hotter than my apartment and the worker behind the counter is sweating profusely: his forehead, his underarms, probably his crotch and his balls, everything. I guess they don't have air conditioning either. Or they've decided to forego it in an effort to save money. Times are tight. Hygienic concerns aside, I order a large pepperoni and ask him how long it'll take.

"I have to finish this other one first. . . so maybe fifteen, twenty minutes?" As opposed to waiting and melting to death, I tell him I'll come back when it's ready.

Avoiding the hustle of the main streets, I light myself a cigarette and decide on a stroll through the nearby residential area. Row upon row of uniform houses, each two storeys tall and made of brown brick. Most of the houses have a small wooden deck at the front, typically with a barbecue and a couple of chairs. Four sets of parents have congregated on one of the decks, talking and laughing while their children play on the front lawn, running around in circles and spraying each other with toy water guns.

The scene reminds me of the first time I met Rachael. We were really young—only twelve or thirteen—and one day after school some classmates and I walked to a friend's house where all the neighbourhood kids were having a water fight. We joined in, and within ten minutes I was completely drenched. Feeling thirsty, I asked my friend where I could get a drink and he pointed to the house next door. There was a patio at the back and I walked up the stairs and opened the sliding door and saw her sitting there in the kitchen, alone, nursing a small bruise on her ankle. Apparently she had tripped while dodging an airborne water balloon. I found some ice in the freezer and wrapped it up in a paper towel and gave it to her to apply to the wound. "Thanks," she said. Then she told me her name was Rachael.

It wasn't long before we were calling each other on a daily basis. Ten-minute phone conversations turned into two-hour marathon sessions. Every Sunday she volunteered at a local children's hospital, and she once complained to me that she had no one to eat lunch with, so I told her I'd meet her in the cafeteria any time she wanted—even though the hospital was an hour's walk from my house and the weather was often cold, rainy and miserable. Still, I was true to my word. I would have taken any excuse to be with her. In many ways we were polar opposites: she was incredibly cheerful, bright, altruistic and always had something to say, whereas I was a shy, bitter, reclusive kid. Yet somehow we connected. Maybe because we could always make each other laugh, no matter how bad things got. I haven't met anybody like that since.

As I'm walking past the children, one of the girls—she can't be more than five—lowers her water gun and waves at me. I hide the cigarette behind my back because I don't want her to see me smoking and then I smile and wave back. Content, she turns around and rejoins the game. I continue down the street and I can hear one of the parents sternly reminding her to put her shoes on.

I wonder what it's like to be one of those parents, to wake up next to the same person every morning, driving around in a family-friendly mid-sized sedan and chasing after a bunch of kids who have infinitely more energy than you, worrying about whether they've eaten enough or washed their hands or remembered to put their shoes on. In a way I pity them because they must be sleep-deprived and mentally exhausted, never having a moment to themselves. But, deep down, I also envy them because their goal is simple: go to work and take care of the family. Nothing else matters. When you're single, the highs are higher and the lows are lower. There's less stability, no consistency, and every day is unpredictable: it could be amazing or it could be awful and either way you have to face it alone.

When the pizza is ready, I carry it to the side of the building and sit down on a pair of wooden steps. I'm absolutely starving. Opening the box, I rip into it as if I haven't eaten in days, burning the roof of my mouth in the process and breathing heavily between bites. Across the street I see a panhandler with a bushy grey beard and a dirty white shirt. He has an upside-down baseball cap placed in front of him and there are probably a few nickels and quarters inside. I figure I owe the homeless a favour after that altercation last night, so when the light changes, I cross the street and approach him.

"Hey I'm sorry, man, I don't have any change, but do you want some pizza?"

"Yeah!" he exclaims. He's more excited than I would have predicted. "Thank you. I'm starving. And it's hot as hell out here."

"I know."

I slump down beside the panhandler with the box on my lap and we both eat a slice while staring out at the passing traffic. Row upon row of uniform cars moving in opposite directions. I can't make out any of the faces behind the windshields due to the reflected sunlight, so every car looks the same. An infinite number.

I think the hardest part of being homeless would be the boredom. No television, internet, movies or video games; entire days spent glancing at the passers-by and hoping they pity you enough to toss a few coins into your hat. I often see homeless men sleeping in the subway tunnels underneath a pile of heavy blankets and they're always by themselves. When I was eight years old, I ran away from home and decided I was going to live under a bridge. I packed a Game Boy, a change of batteries, a sleeping bag, a spoon, and several cans of Chef Boyardee Ravioli—I figured that would last me for at least three or four months. Within two hours I said "forget this" and went home to laze on the couch and watch cartoons again. I was so goddamn bored under that bridge.

Later, in high school, I would often skip an entire day of classes and drift along the streets from nine o'clock in the morning until three in the afternoon. The teachers all knew I was playing hooky, but they didn't care because I managed to score higher than the other students despite my poor attendance. And my attendance was very poor: I missed over two hundred classes in my senior year. Sometimes I just couldn't take it: another boring day at school surrounded by asshole teenagers. I had zits on my face, long hair and a lanky body I hadn't quite grown into, and the other kids made sure I knew about it daily. So I would sneak away to a library to read books or to an art gallery to look at black-and-white photographs or wander downtown to find an alleyway to sleep in. With little money my options were fairly limited. I felt like an outcast, cowering behind dumpsters and smoking Colt cigars while huddling beneath my winter jacket. I fantasized about becoming a famous rock star and writing a song about being poor and homeless like Kurt Cobain did with "Something in the Way." I could play the guitar, but my technique was all mechanical; I had no natural talent as a musician and the lyrics I scribbled down were hackneyed and meaningless. Good musicians can wear their emotions on their sleeves, and I was never able to do that. In the end, it was just me outside in the cold with little more than a pipe dream to keep me warm.

Not surprisingly, that was about the time I started drinking. There was a store not far from where I lived where I'd buy beer whenever I had the cash. The old man behind the counter must've been severely near-sighted because he never asked me for ID. Or maybe he just took pity on me. From then on I always kept a few bottles of beer and liquor in my backpack and used them whenever I needed them. I drank behind gas stations, in empty parking lots, on playgrounds, in the backseat of cars, even in the school cafeteria on one occasion. I never want to be homeless. But the way things are going it's a definite possibility. I should be nice to these panhandlers—I might be begging alongside them someday.

The panhandler and I are sitting side by side on the pavement, still staring out at the passing traffic in silence while we chew and digest and breathe. As soon as he's finished eating, he asks, "Can I have another one?"

"Yeah, for sure." I rip off a slice and hand it to him.

"Thanks. Don't worry. I won't take any more from you."

"Are you sure? There's plenty to go around."

"No, that's okay. You go on now. And as soon as I win the lotto, I'm gonna pay you back!"

On the walk home I take a short detour and find a park bench to lie on and look up at the sky. I'm relieved my stomach doesn't hurt anymore; it probably won't hurt again until tomorrow morning. It's an awful feeling, to be paralyzed by hunger. Every day, for the first few hours after waking, my stomach is so sore from the alcohol that the mere thought of food makes me nauseous. If I tried to eat, my body would immediately reject it, and at the same time it growls, it moans and it aches because it needs food. I have to starve myself because I'm physically *unable* to eat.

I've lost fifteen pounds since last year.

Thirteen

When the mail arrives through the door slot there's a letter from the Faculty of Law at Queen's University, and I know by the size of the envelope that it's a rejection letter. When a school accepts you, they usually send a handbook, a catalogue or a big academic calender inside a large yellow envelope. This envelope is small and white. I tear it open and read: *We regret to inform you we can only offer enrolment to a certain number of applicants and your application for the fall semester was not accepted.* They encourage me to try again next year. More rejection letters will be coming soon—this is just the beginning. I rip the letter into several pieces and then toss it into the trash. I wouldn't make a good lawyer anyway. There's also a note from the superintendent reminding me that my rent from June is overdue. I'll have to put it on my credit card.

My phone vibrates and I check the display to see it's my friend Nikki calling. I met her through Craig a few months back and she often comes out drinking with us. Nikki has rich parents and lives in a loft downtown, so she doesn't have to worry about work or money. Instead, she spends most of her time cooking, blogging, taking theatre classes and studying to become an optician. I've never seen her wear the same thing twice and her outfit is always eccentric and colourful. She's attractive, but she only sleeps with men after they've dated her for several months, so my friends and I have given up on that endeavour. Now, we consider her a part of the group, a fifth member, one of the guys.

I never saw her as a potential mate, anyway, because she's blonde—not that I have anything against blondes, mind you, but they, for whatever reason, never seem to have any interest in me. Not sure why. I've hooked up with at least fifty women in my life and I can't remember *one* that was blonde.

"Nikki, what's up?"

"Hey! How's it going?"

"Real good," I say sarcastically. "You?"

"I'm great. Sorry I couldn't hang out with you guys last night. I hear Silverchest *killed*!"

"Yeah, she beat those trash cans pretty good. . . ."

"Cool! Okay. So. Listen. I'm meeting a friend of mine for drinks in about an hour and we're gonna be in your neck of the woods. Wanna come?"

"Hmm . . . I don't know. I'm supposed to meet up with Natalie tonight and I was hoping to be at least *somewhat* sober—"

"Forget that! Forget that ho! C'mon, you don't have to drink much. And my friend Charlotte is really cool. You'll like her."

"Alright," I sigh. "I'll make an appearance."

"Cool! We're going to the Duke of Kent north of Yonge and Eglinton. Be there at four."

The Duke of Kent markets itself as an English pub and it has all of the usual features: a wooden bar with golden pillars, yellow walls, red and green carpeting, soccer on the television and bangers and mash on the menu. They sell pints of draught beer primarily to an older, dedicated clientele, all of whom seem to know each other, so I feel right at home hunched over the counter on a plush red stool and sipping a gin-and-tonic while waiting for Nikki to arrive. They're even playing "Smokestack Lightning" by Howlin' Wolf over the speakers—a favourite blues song of mine. I sit there and drink and stare at the soccer game on the television mounted onto the wall and Germany is playing Uruguay and the score is tied. A large group of devoted, face-painted football fans have shown up to watch the match and they're hooting and hollering at the screen anytime a player does *anything*—passes, shoots, slide tackles, anything. I holler along with them on particularly egregious plays.

Beside me there's a man and a woman in their mid-thirties perched on stools ignoring the game. The woman is droning on incessantly, complaining about her ex-boyfriend while the guy looks longingly into her eyes with his chin cradled in the palm of his hand. She's loud and obnoxious and he's hanging on her every word, nodding and smiling at all the right moments, but I can tell by her body language that she has absolutely no interest in him: her feet are positioned away to the side, she's leaning back, she doesn't maintain eye contact or mirror any of his gestures and she barely looks at his face. I actually feel sorry for the guy: this poor bastard has probably been told his whole life that *all he has to do* is listen to women and they'll instantly fall in love with him. It's a little more complicated than that. This particular woman is used to having everybody listen to her because she's pretty and overly talkative. Simply listening to her won't work. With somebody like that, you have to be energetic, spontaneous, keep the conversation moving equally in both directions. Stand out. Be confident. Rachael taught me that. It's the quiet, introverted ones that you really have to listen to. You should ask them questions and listen to the answers because they actually have something to say. Women are infinitely more interesting than men, but not this one, and this poor bastard doesn't have a prayer.

I'm so distracted by their one-way conversation and the unruly soccer fans in the background that I don't notice Nikki coming into the pub. She walks up behind me and squeezes me on the shoulders. "Hey there, cutie!" Her hair is slightly shorter and darker at the roots than the last time I saw her and it perfectly frames her face.

"What's up? Where's your friend?" I ask.

"She's on her way. Wanna grab a table?"

"Sure."

When I tell the bartender I'm moving, she stops and does a double-take and then suddenly recognizes me. Her brow furrows and she asks me if I'm going to be "drinking a lot tonight" because apparently the last time I was in here I passed out in an alcove and they had to pour water on my face to wake me up. I apologize and leave her a good tip and then meet Nikki at a round table at the back of the pub. We've barely taken our seats, but she's already eager to tell me everything about Charlotte. "She's originally from Winnipeg, but now she goes to school at U of T. She's doing her undergrad in science. Biology, I think."

"That's cool. I love science."

"She hates chemistry though."

"Why? What's wrong with chemistry?"

"She doesn't like it. So don't bring it up."

"But what if I *have* to?"

She laughs. "Don't!"

"I was gonna ask her about bunsen burners and shit. . . ."

She laughs again. "Just don't!"

Moments later, Charlotte wanders in through the centre of the pub and Nikki sees her and waves at her and then we slide over and she takes a seat across from me. I introduce myself and shake her hand. She has a pretty round face, long brown hair and a bright purple top, but she seems a little shy. Nikki and Charlotte talk about their classes and mention a few mutual acquaintances, people I don't know, and then I ask her about where she's from and what she's doing in Toronto and she tells me about her program at school before eventually excusing herself to go to the washroom.

When she's out of sight, Nikki turns to me and says, "So! Whaddya think?"

"She seems nice."

Nikki smiles and says coyly, "Cool."

"Wait, are you trying to set us up or something?"

"Maybe . . ."

" 'Cause that's the last thing I need right now."

"It's exactly what you need, Ethan! It'll be good for her, too. She has a boyfriend, but I really don't like him—"

"She has a boyfriend?"

"Yeah, but I really don't like him."

"It's not your call!"

"No, seriously, he's pretty weird. . . ."

"So, what, you want me to try to break them up?"

"No! I don't think they'll last much longer anyway."

"Well, fingers crossed!" I say sarcastically. Then I take another sip of gin and loudly inhale before adding, "This is *kinda* fucked up."

"You need a girlfriend, Ethan. I know you. You're not like Craig or Jeff, no matter how much you might try to be. Don't get me wrong. I love those guys. But they're assholes. You're not an asshole. You're the kinda guy who would rather stay at home and curl up on the couch and watch movies. You should be in a relationship."

"No, Nikki, I shouldn't. I need to get my shit together."

"Ah, your shit's fine."

"My shit sucks!"

Charlotte returns just in time to hear me shout that last line, but she doesn't say anything about it. She takes her seat and we order another round of drinks and then the conversation gradually veers toward me and what I've been up to lately. I tell her about my law school applications, how I'm between jobs at the moment because the economy is slow and businesses aren't hiring, and then I talk about my useless bachelor degree and how I probably should have studied something other than English and History. I use a joke I heard from Larry David about how my degree is "only good for solving crossword puzzles" and she laughs and in the corner of my eye I see Nikki flashing me a knowing smile, as if to say, "See?" But the sparks aren't exactly flying; I'm too hungover and thinking about Natalie and wondering if I'll actually get to see her again tonight.

About half an hour later I begin to feel bored and find myself daydreaming, glancing at the soccer game and pondering other things while they continue to converse. Suddenly, Charlotte asks me a question about my astrological sign and it catches me off guard.

"Huh? Oh, I'm a Libra."

"Ah, a libra," she repeats. Then she turns to Nikki and says, "They're all about balance."

"Balance . . . that's me, alright."

She doesn't detect the sarcasm.

"My boyfriend's a Scorpio," Charlotte says, "which is great because I'm a Pisces and we're really compatible with Scorpios."

"All the Scorpios I've met have been kinda weird," Nikki mutters.

Astrology. They talk about it like it's a fact. I know I shouldn't debate the issue with someone I've just met, but I feel compelled to play the devil's advocate here—plus, I sense an opportunity to liven up the conversation. "Wait, you don't actually believe that shit, do you?"

"It's not shit," Charlotte recoils. "It's true."

"You think giant balls of gas millions of light-years away are gonna determine whether you and your boyfriend get along or not?"

Charlotte scoffs. "It's more complicated than that. It's about their position and relation to the earth relative to when you were born."

"Do you believe in psychics too? Ghosts? Angels?"

"Yes?"

"What about unicorns?"

"Well, not unicorns—"

"Why not? What's the difference?"

"Ethan," she says condescendingly, "there are some people who have been *proven* to be psychic."

"Like who?"

"Lots of people. They help with police investigations."

"Well, I've read about this guy named Randi who's been offering a million dollars to anyone who can prove they have *any* kind of psychic power for, like, thirty years, and not one person has been able to claim the prize."

"So? That doesn't mean psychics don't exist."

"Kinda odd though, don't ya think?"

"What about when you get déjà vu? Or when the phone rings and you know who's calling?"

"Déjà vu is caused by a glitch in the synapse of your brain—"

"No it isn't!"

"—and the phone thing is just intuition."

"It isn't!"

"You're supposed to be a scientist!"

I notice Nikki is frowning and obviously irritated by the direction the conversation has taken; she tries to intervene and change the subject, but we ignore her.

"You study science," I say. "You're supposed to look for evidence."

"There *is* evidence!"

"No there isn't."

"So, what, you don't believe in anything? You're an atheist?"

"I'm reserving judgement on that one."

"Ah ha."

"Let me put it this way: if there is a God, I'm pretty sure he doesn't give a shit about us."

"He does. He does care. Listen, when my grandpa got lung cancer, my family and I prayed every single day. The doctors all said he would only live for, like, a couple months, and that was years ago. He's still alive and well today."

"And you think a higher power had something to do with that?"

"Yes! Of course I do."

"Then why didn't God help all the people who died in Haiti a few months back? Is your grandpa more important than them?"

"I don't know? Maybe He is helping them."

"So He causes a giant earthquake just for kicks?"

Charlotte sighs. "Mysterious ways. I think it's above our comprehension. He tests us and makes us face adversity in order to make us better people."

"Well, He's doing a real bang-up job then, huh? People are really great these days, aren't they? And how come He only acts when nobody's watching? According to you, He can heal people, but He won't heal an amputee because then we'd actually be able to *see* it. He's like Woody in *Toy Story* . . . He goes limp anytime we look at him."

"It's not like that, Ethan."

While I'm trying to articulate my next point, I pause for a moment to survey the pub. The raucous, face-painted soccer fans are yelling at the television, taking shots of tequila and licking the salt off of their hands while a few old-timers keel over the bar counter, working on their sixth pint of the day at five o'clock in the afternoon. Then I return my attention to Charlotte and roll my index finger in a circular motion around the room. "You see 'God' anywhere around here?"

Charlotte doesn't answer.

"Face it. We're on our own. The world is too complicated for God. He's just an old, antiquated idea that prevents us from solving our real problems."

"So you think the whole universe is one big coincidence then?"

"Pretty much."

"Then what's the meaning of it all?"

I shrug my shoulders. "There is no meaning."

"Oh that's such a cop-out!" She turns to Nikki and adds, "I'm so glad Drew isn't an atheist. It'd be such a turn-off."

"A turn-off? And your boyfriend's name is *Drew*? Oh, for fuck's sake. . . ."

Charlotte ignores my snide remark and continues, "I could never be with someone who didn't believe in *something*."

Nikki shakes her head and turns away from us, no doubt disappointed that Charlotte and I won't be walking down the aisle anytime soon. But I actually liked debating with her; it's not often people give you a chance to wax philosophical on God and the meaning of life. Nobody ever seems to ask the big questions anymore because they're so afraid of offending someone. Having said that, I hope I didn't offend her too much. She seems like a decent person.

We sip our drinks and there's a long, uncomfortable hush, so I decide to break the silence. "So, Charlotte . . . what's your favourite noble gas?"

Nikki grins at me in spite of herself. "I kinda like helium. It makes your voice sound all funny."

"I like boron," I say confidently.

"Boron's not a noble gas," Charlotte sighs.

"I know it isn't . . . but it still gets me *hard*."

Pleased with myself, I take another swig of gin and then count the minutes before I can go home and call Natalie.

FOURTEEN

Natalie doesn't answer when I call her, so I wait twenty minutes and try again. Still no response. Is she cancelling on me? The least she could do is let me know. I'm debating whether or not to leave a brief voicemail message when suddenly I receive a text from Scott that reads: *Hey! I bought some cocaine last night. Wanna give it a shot? Craig is here. Come over. Yaow!*

Cocaine? Where'd he get cocaine? I've never known him to indulge in any drug aside from marijuana. And hash. And mushrooms. But never cocaine. I decide to give him a call.

"Hey! Reid! You get my message? I have coke!"

"Really? How?"

"I ran into this guy last night after you left and I asked him if he had any weed and he said he did, so I paid him the money and he goes, 'Wait, sorry, I actually don't have any weed, but do you want this coke instead?' And I was like, 'Okay.' And now I have coke."

"Nice."

"I eventually found some weed, too."

"Attaboy."

"So, you coming over? Craig's already here."

"I don't know. I'm kinda waiting on a phone call."

"Well, why don't you come here and pre-drink with us while you wait? I can give you a ride downtown after. You won't have to pay the subway fare. That's a saving of three dollars, my friend."

". . . Alright, I'm on my way."

About an hour later, the three of us are perched around a glass table in Scott's living room. Like mine, his apartment is a mess: dirty clothes and various pieces of sporting equipment are discarded haphazardly on the floor alongside an array of marijuana paraphernalia. We sip on liquor and smoke cigarettes until Scott finally unveils a ziplock bag full of white powder—hopefully he bought actual cocaine and not baking soda—and pours it onto a mirror in the centre of the table.

"Don't we need a razor blade or something?" Craig asks.

"No, it's already cut," says Scott. "But we need a credit card to divvy it up." I retrieve a library card from my wallet and toss it over to him, watching as he starts pushing and sorting the white powder into six separate lines.

"I've never done this before," Craig says, shifting in his chair. "Someone else go first."

"I'll go," I say. I've snorted cocaine on several occasions, but never this early in the evening or this sober. It's a drug that usually only makes an appearance at the end of a night, typically in a bathroom stall or at somebody's house after the bars have closed. I rarely buy it for myself because it's far too expensive; however, there was one time during a particularly heavy bender when I wandered into a busy intersection at three o'clock in the morning and shouted, "Hey! Somebody sell me some coke!" Ten seconds later, a man in a thick black jacket obliged me. There were two police cars in the immediate area, but somehow they failed to notice our transaction. Or maybe they didn't care. Either way, I was lucky.

I roll up a five-dollar bill until it's taut, then insert it into my right nostril and lean forward so that the bill is hovering over the line. Closing off the rest of my nose with a free finger, I inhale as hard as possible, like a vacuum, not stopping until the powder is completely gone. The feeling hits me instantly like a shotgun blast to the brain: a burning, euphoric rush that I've never experienced before. My mind elevates and feels lighter, as if it were full of air. And I want more. I desperately want more.

"How is it?" Craig asks.

"Man, I love it," I say, rubbing my nose and sniffling. "You feel it immediately. I get why this stuff is so addictive." I stand up from the table and start pacing around the room; my heart is beating faster and I'm overcome with adrenaline and I can't stop clapping my hands together.

"Okay, my turn," says Scott. I pass him the bill and he lowers his head toward the mirror and slowly breathes it in. His face comes up quickly and there's white powder all over the edge of his nostril and he starts coughing and laughing. "Shit! That fuckin' burns!" He hurriedly wipes his nose from side to side. "I don't know if I feel anything though."

"I do," I say. "If I were rich, or if this stuff were any cheaper, I'd do it all the time."

"It could just be me. I didn't get high the first time I smoked weed either."

Craig points at the mirror. "Or maybe that's just sugar?"

"Nah, it's real," I say. "Give it a shot, man."

"I'll try anything once," he mumbles as he bends over the mirror. He inhales deeply and it takes him longer to finish, but the line eventually disappears. "Wow, that does burn. But it feels kinda cool."

"Alright, let me try another one," I say, grabbing the bill out of his hand. I repeat the process and the rush feels the same, albeit with less intensity.

"You can have my second line too," he says. "I'm good."

Without lifting my head from the table, I go in for another hit and I hear Scott yell, "Save some for me, cokehead!" After we finish the remnants of white dust, we celebrate by rolling a joint and smoking it outside on the balcony. Then we put on our shoes and leave the apartment, ready to paint the town red.

FIFTEEN

The flashing lights and swirling neon signs of Toronto's entertainment district blur and bombard me as I peer through the backseat window of our green Pontiac Sunfire. Loud shoegaze rock pumps through the speakers and the heavy bass vibrates the car as the singer moans about space girls and sunsets—apparently it's a band called Swervedriver. The aural stimulation, combined with the dizzying high of several narcotics, makes me feel as if I'm in another world; I can see an entire city block for a single moment and then nothing at all, just an overwhelming array of synthetic colour and illumination. The city ebbs and flows above me and all I can do is watch in awe.

Scott is behind the wheel, and at one point he fishtails through a busy intersection to avoid colliding with an oncoming vehicle and the incident triggers an old memory. It's a cold, quiet night in November and I'm teaching Rachael how to drive in an empty parking lot. We're both seventeen years old and I recently earned my driver's licence. I climb into the passenger seat while she places her hands on the steering wheel, and then I tell her about the pedals, the lights, the mirrors and the turn signals while she nods and pretends to listen to my boring tutorial. Then, without warning, she suddenly presses her foot down on the gas and we start speeding through the lot. The car keeps accelerating. We're going so fast. We're running out of room and I begin to panic. I tell her to slow down and she just looks at me and smiles. Then she nonchalantly slams on the brakes and jerks the wheel all the way to the left, causing the car to spin around one-hundred-and-eighty degrees. The tires drag against the asphalt and the brakes squeal and whine and then the hood rocks forward before the vehicle finally juts to a stop. I nearly have a heart attack. I get out of the car and run around to the driver's side door and pull it open and she's already laughing so hard that I can't help but laugh too. We're both keeling over. "I should probably drive," I tell her. She undoes her seatbelt, falls out of the car and gives me a hug before walking back to the passenger's side. Then the memory cuts out.

The sun has almost set. We gracefully shuffle and veer through the streets on our way to rescue Doc from the corporate hell that is Starbucks. When we arrive he's already waiting for us on the curb dressed in black, with his traditionally unkempt hair combed neatly to the side. We pull up beside him and roll down the windows and then taunt and jeer at him for having chlamydia.

"Oh very funny," he says.

Doc climbs into the backseat and we light another joint and then hand him a beer as a way of welcoming him back into our world. He opens the can and inhales the joint and smoke tumbles from his lungs, enveloping the entire car. We take turns breathing it in and passing the joint around until there's nothing left but burnt paper and ash. At Scott's insistence, we save the roach for him. As I'm passing the remnants up to Craig, I notice the air freshener dangling from his rearview mirror: it looks like Jesus cradling a small car in his arms. I ask Scott what it smells like and he yells, "Lemons!"

"Alright, so where are we going?" someone asks.

"Well, I've gotta drop off the car," Scott replies. "Then I figured we'd subway over to the Annex and see what's up."

"Fine by me."

"What about you, Reid? You coming with us?"

"Yeah, I might as well. She's probably not gonna call."

"Awesome."

"Okay," says Doc, "but I gotta go home and change my clothes first. I wanna wear my 'Dubya' shirt tonight."

Doc owns a t-shirt with a portrait of George W. Bush looking brave and steadfast, staring straight into the wind, and underneath there's a caption that reads *NO MISTAKES*. He wears it as often as possible—not because he actually admires the former president, but because he likes to anger people.

"Sure," says Scott. "You gotta be quick though."

"Uh huh," Doc replies. Then he scans the interior of the car and asks, "Hey, what year is this jalopy?"

"It's a two-thousand-one."

"Man, I can't believe I have a shittier car than you."

"I make more money, asshole!" Scott replies. It's true: Scott makes more money than anyone I know, yet he still can't afford to buy a decent car. What he does for a living? None of us know for sure, but it's some miscellaneous office job with computers and information systems. We don't really talk about our career aspirations—to be honest, I don't think these guys have any. They seem completely satisfied with the status quo—in other words, living paycheque to paycheque in cramped, one-bedroom apartments. As long as they have enough money to get drunk on Saturdays, they don't care.

"Whatever," says Doc. "My new car is gonna put yours to shame."

"What's wrong with the Widowmaker?" I ask.

"It's too old and shitty and it's gonna explode," he replies. "I want a car with a giant engine that shakes the earth, one that inspires fear in the hearts of my enemies." He blows more smoke from his mouth and adds, "Anyway, let's hurry the hell up. I've gotta get *way* drunker than this."

We drop off the car at Doc's apartment and then hop on the subway at Dundas Square. When our train arrives at Bathurst Station, we walk outside to witness a crowd of people assembling on the street corner and watching a nearby building burn to the ground. Flames consume the entire structure and shoot out through an open window on the second floor. There are no sirens, no fire engines, only gawkers and on-lookers smiling and laughing, snapping photos with their cellphones and appreciating that they are, for once, seeing something out of the ordinary happen in front of their very eyes. I'm no different: I hold a phone an inch from my face and click the camera over and over again, making slight adjustments in the angle, experimenting with the flash, trying it on, trying it off, zooming in and out.

Scott is particularly impressed. "Holy shit!" he says. "That's cool. Do you think somebody died?" Then he tells me a story of how he saw a man get struck and killed by a vehicle when he was vacationing in Boston. "It was right in front of me!" he exclaims, using his hands to illustrate the angle at which the car veered into him.

I feel as if I should call somebody. Let the authorities know. I consider running over to the building to see if anybody's inside. Maybe they need my help. Indifference, however, wins out. Wins out over me, my friends, and every other spectator on that street corner. I simply stand there and watch it burn.

"Well that sucks," Doc says as he exhales a long puff of cigarette smoke.

Scott pats me on the back. "Come on. Let's get hammered. I got the first round."

We leave the fire and walk eastward along Bloor Street toward Lee's Palace, a popular music venue for touring bands. A long lineup of people are leaning against the colourful mural on the wall by the entrance waiting to get inside. We join the back of the line and a few young guys follow behind us. They look like they're still in high school; when I ask how old they are, they admit they're only seventeen, but they're going to try to sneak into the club by greasing the bouncer.

"Why do you wanna get in there so badly?" I ask. "You know it's just loud music and overpriced drinks, right?"

One of the boys looks at me with a blank expression on his face and says plainly, "What else are we gonna do on a Saturday night?"

The line moves forward and we wish the boys good luck and then show the bouncers our IDs and walk inside. Instead of following the hallway straight into the main room, we ascend a black staircase with black walls to a large black room with bright lights and a dance floor where two hundred people are dancing to "Transmission" by Joy Division. I've never heard Joy Division in a club before and I'm impressed by their choice of music. Leaving my jacket on a bench, I notice some of the female patrons look quite young. I warn my friends to be careful.

"Ah, I'll be fine," Doc assures me.

I watch as my three friends approach the bar and return a minute later with a bottle of beer in each hand. Scott buys me a double gin-and-tonic and we stand and drink, gradually gathering up the courage to join the crowd on the dance floor. It doesn't take Doc very long: he jumps into the crowd after a few sips of beer and Scott follows closely behind. They immediately start dancing next to a group of girls while Craig and I lean against the bar and spectate. I wonder if he's thinking the same thing I am: people look really stupid when they're dancing. Unfortunately, I'll soon be out there too, fumbling around with the rest of them.

If Natalie's not coming tonight, if she's not even answering my calls, then this entire expedition is a waste of time. As if he's reading my mind, Craig asks, "So, what happened to Natalie tonight?"

"I don't know. I called, but I haven't heard back."

"That sucks," he says, casually drinking his beer. "She seems kinda flakey, man. Like, I look at her sometimes, and she doesn't seem to react to things like a normal person. More like a robot. Anyway, I wouldn't take it too personally."

"Screw it. I'm gonna try to have fun here tonight."

"Good call. Who needs a girlfriend these days anyway? Porn is amazing."

"That's true."

"I downloaded this one last night that I'm *pretty* excited about. This guy's on a golf course, right, and he's getting a lesson from this chick, and she starts talking about his three-wood and—"

"I really wish she'd call me though," I interrupt.

"Well, wish in one hand, shit in the other, dude."

"Huh. Maybe that's my problem. . . ."

"What is?"

"Maybe I've gotta stop *wishing* and *shitting* on my hands all the time."

Craig laughs. "That's the spirit."

I finish my drink, slam the cup on the counter and order another one. When I turn around, I'm surprised to find Nikki standing right in front of me. She grabs me by the collar and shakes me, spilling gin-and-tonic onto my shoes.

"Hey! I'm drinkin' here!" I yell.

"Ethan Reid! What the hell was that today?"

"What's she talking about?" Craig asks me.

"We went to the Duke a couple hours ago," Nikki explains, "and I introduced him to Charlotte and he totally scared her off!"

"That's surprising," Craig deadpans.

"Oh, c'mon," I say. "It's not my fault. She's a goddamn Pisces!"

Nikki sneers at me and then glances down at my wristwatch and asks me what time it is.

"I don't know."

"Tell me!"

"No, seriously. My watch is busted. Look."

I show her that the hands aren't moving.

"Then why are you still wearing it?"

"To remind myself to get it fixed. Besides, it makes me look cool."

Nikki lets out a sigh of frustration and shouts, "You're all over the map!" Then she suddenly perks up and taps me on the forearm. "Oh! By the way, I was talking to a friend of mine on Facebook and she said she saw you at a party on Thursday. Apparently you were *totally* wasted. She said you smashed an iPod on the pavement and then kicked it into a sewer grate."

"Really?"

"Yeah!"

"Huh. So *that's* where that went."

Sixteen

The wind is blowing harder now and a few smokers have gathered on the sidewalk, standing in a circle like a pack of hobos at a burn barrel. In the midst of the herd, I recognize a girl from my campus pub: her name is Caitlyn and she works there as a waitress. Naturally, I met her when I was drinking scotch between classes. She graduated in April, from what I heard, and I didn't think I would ever see her again.

I like Caitlyn, but she's a bit of an idiot. She has no interest in contemporary books or movies or music and she spends most of her time watching old sitcoms like *Perfect Strangers* and *Coach*. In her defence, though, I've met thousands of people in my life and I've found that a person's taste in art and entertainment is usually irrelevant. I once heard somebody say "What matters is *what you like*, not *what you are like*," and trust me, that's complete horseshit. Don't believe it for a second. I have a theory that a successful friendship, or a relationship of any kind, is based on three simple things: chemistry, circumstance and longevity.

Chemistry refers to the undefinable biological forces that attract people together. Sense of humour, friendliness, pheromones—they're all a part of chemistry. Good chemistry doesn't necessarily require common interests, which is why people from entirely different cultures and backgrounds can become friends almost instantly upon meeting. And chemistry can build over time. Rachael and I had it in spades. But chemistry isn't always enough—you also need the circumstances to be in your favour. You have to work at the same job, or go to the same school, or have the same friends, or live in the same city, or be single at the same time. If the circumstances don't match up, then the relationship probably won't last; in fact, a change of circumstance is usually what causes people to drift apart. And then there's longevity: some people are your friends simply because you've known them for such a long time. Even if you no longer have anything in common, you can still reminisce and talk about years past and stay bonded out of a sense of loyalty or obligation—family being a good example of that, too.

My point is: I don't fault Caitlyn for her horrible taste in books and movies and music because *it doesn't matter*. The chemistry is there. We find things to talk about. We tell each other stories and discuss people we know and current events and our plans for the future and the conversation always flows easily. Besides, she's attractive and I wouldn't mind jumping her bones.

"Hey, do you have a light?" I ask.

She notices me and her eyes widen with recognition and then she embraces me with a lazy hug. "Hey man! What're you doing here?"

"Ah, my friends dragged me out. I was supposed to meet up with somebody, but they didn't show. What about you?"

"A friend of mine just got engaged, so a bunch of us are out celebrating. But yeah, good to see you! You're done school now, huh?"

"Not quite. Still trying to figure out what I wanna do."

"That's cool. You gotta add me on Facebook!"

"I will. Real soon."

"Good. Do it." Then she looks down at her shoes and fidgets awkwardly as if she's cold before saying, "Do you wanna sit down somewhere? I've been on my feet all day."

"Yeah, sure."

I follow Caitlyn through an alleyway at the side of the building where we find a short concrete wall and a wooden fence to lean against while we smoke. She tells me she's going on a trip to Europe in August, and when I ask her where, she confuses Denmark with the Netherlands. I don't call her on it—she'll find out soon enough when she lands in Copenhagen. We talk for several minutes and she touches me on the arm when I make her laugh and I'm beginning to think she might actually like me. Or maybe she's just drunk.

"So, what about you?" she asks. "What're you doing for the rest of the summer?"

"Job hunting, mostly. But it's not going too well. I just wanna find a job I don't hate going to everyday, y'know?"

"Mm-hmm. Any idea where you wanna work?"

"I'd take anything, really. I don't have any marketable skills, though. Or unmarketable, for that matter." I shrug and haul back on my cigarette. Thinking about the future makes me anxious. I try to avoid it entirely.

"Too bad we're not hiring at the pub. They really cut back on hours during the summer. It'd be fun if you worked there, too."

"Yeah, I could bartend. Or serve. I've seen what you guys do and it doesn't look too hard," I say jokingly.

"Hey! It is hard! Especially when you get some asshole trying to walk out on the bill. I had one the other night. Cost me, like, fifty bucks. That comes out of my pay. They expect me to keep tabs on every table. I'm like, 'Install a camera or something.' But no, they basically want me to serve *and* work security."

"Sounds like they need another bouncer."

"Well yeah, among other things."

"I could do that. I mean, I'm pretty intimidating." I flex my biceps and she laughs and then halfheartedly punches me on the shoulder. "Be honest. You're intimidated right now."

"Terrified!" she says.

I was so dispirited by Natalie's no-show tonight, but Caitlyn here might save the day. We could have a few drinks and then take a taxi back to her place and watch *Coach*. Or, at the very least, I can get her phone number and take her out at a later date. The possibilities are endless. Things are looking up.

"So, you got any plans this week?" I ask.

"Yeah! Big plans. I'm *so* looking forward to it. On Thursday, my boyfriend's band is playing at this house party and . . ."

As soon as she says the word "boyfriend," I tune out. Girls always drop that word into a conversation so callously, with such indifference, as if this homely-looking son of a bitch standing right next to them couldn't possibly be interested. I should've known. Every girl my age has a boyfriend. Boyfriends! I hate them more than any other demographic on earth. Under normal circumstances, I'd conceal my disappointment, continue to make eye contact and laugh and smile and nod at all the socially-required moments until I could politely excuse myself from the conversation. But tonight has been exceptionally fucked up and I don't have the patience to perform the usual song and dance routine.

"You have a boyfriend, huh?" I interrupt her.

"Yup! Been together almost six months now."

"Any . . . friction there?"

"Any what?"

"Friction. Between you two."

While initially confused by the question, she eventually answers, "No, things are going pretty good. I like him a lot."

"So, you're probably gonna be together for a while, huh?"

"I hope so. . . ."

"Ah, crap."

I drop my cigarette onto the ground and stomp it and then start walking away.

"Ethan? Where are you going?"

"Sorry, I gotta go . . . take a shit."

Back in Lee's Palace, I leave the bathroom stall and wash my hands and then return to the bar upstairs where I immediately spot two of my friends on the dance floor. Craig is in the corner making out with a short blonde girl, possibly underage, while Doc is grinding his hips into another teenager who could be her twin. Rather than interrupt them, I go to the bar and order three shots of Jägermeister. The bartender nods and arranges three plastic cups in a row and then fills them to the brim and I pay him the money. As soon as his back is turned, I drink all three shots one after the other. By this point in the evening my taste buds are so numb that the shots go down like water. I push the empty cups forward and then momentarily rest my chin on the countertop between my folded arms, disappointed by Natalie and jealous of the fact that Caitlyn's boyfriend has his own rock band.

As I'm standing there brooding, I'm suddenly approached by a short, stalky, bald-headed bouncer who gives me a hard tap on the shoulder. He's shaped like a perfect sphere—a goddamn *orb*—and he has a gold earring in his left ear. "You can't stay here, man. You gotta go."

"What? Why?"

"You were sleeping. Can't have that. You gotta go."

"I wasn't sleeping! I put my head down for, like, five seconds! I'm fully awake!"

"Doesn't matter. You gotta go." I can tell by the stern expression on his face that he's not going to budge. When bouncers want you out of their club, there's little you can do to persuade them otherwise. For a moment, I consider pushing him so that he'll roll away, but I refrain.

"Fine, let me get my coat," I say reluctantly. He follows me to the front bench and watches me put on my jacket, and then I walk down the stairs and out onto Bloor Street as he closes the door behind me. It's surprisingly colder and windier than it was earlier in the evening, and the crowd of smokers who were here only minutes earlier have all but dispersed, although a few stragglers still remain.

Suddenly, I feel a vibration in my jacket's inner pocket and reach inside. My phone is ringing. It's Natalie.

"Hello?" I answer.

"Hey! What's up?"

"Not much! I'm downtown on Bloor. What about you?"

"We're just leaving now. Sorry I didn't call you earlier! I had to work later than I thought I would. Me and my co-workers are on our way to Sneaky Dee's, if you wanna meet us there."

"Yeah, sure. I'm pretty close now. Probably be there in ten?"

"Sounds good! See ya then."

As soon as I hang up, I immediately dial Scott's number to let him know what happened and where to meet me. The phone rings. "Hello?" His voice faintly reverberates over the sound of dance music in the background.

"Hey! It's Reid!" I shout.

"Reid! Why are you calling me? Man, this chick is smokin'! She's Joe Frazier! And she said she'll do whatever I *want*!" He's clearly intoxicated and stumbles over his words.

"Scott! Listen to me! I got kicked out of the bar, so—"

"You what? Your phone is echoing."

"I got kicked out, so you're gonna have to meet me at—"

"Why'd you get kicked out?"

"Just shut up and listen! Meet me at Sneaky Dee's, okay?"

"Man, you gotta stop getting kicked outta things—"

"I know. But listen. I'm gonna—"

"What?"

"I said I'm on my way to—"

"I can't hear you!"

"I SAID MEET ME AT SNEAKY DEE'S, YOU ASS-HOLE!" I scream into the phone. A couple of concerned passers-by glare at me as if I'm off my medication.

"He's being an asshole," I quietly assure them.

SEVENTEEN

At the intersection of Bathurst and Bloor I hop on a streetcar heading south. It's overflowing with people, so I stay at the front and hold onto the metal bar until I get off at College. Sneaky Dee's is on the corner, and its green, spaced-out bull sign is hard to miss. The building is divided into two sections: the first floor is a Tex-Mex restaurant specializing in large platters of enchiladas, quesadillas, nachos and refried beans with a kitchen that stays open until the early hours of the morning, long after the bars have closed. Upstairs, there's a small club complete with a stage and dance floor and tonight they're playing upbeat music from the fifties and sixties. It's very warm when I get to the top of the stairs and a haze of sweat and steam seems to emanate from the wooden floor like a sauna. I pay a five-dollar cover fee and then walk inside and immediately spot Natalie standing at the bar by herself waiting to order. I sidle up beside her as the opening guitar riff to "Cherry Cherry" begins to flow from the sound system.

"Man, this song got me through some tough times," I dead-pan, leaning against the counter with my eyes aimed straight forward.

"Really?" she says without turning her head. "You're a big Neil Diamond fan, huh?"

"Oh God yes. He changed my life."

She laughs and then we say hello and she kisses me on the cheek. "I'm glad you came. Come on, let's dance. I'll teach you how to foxtrot or something."

"Don't you wanna get a drink first?"

She grabs me by the hand and starts pulling me onto the dance floor. "Nah, I'm already buzzed! Come on!"

Natalie chaperones me through a sea of people until we're somewhere in the middle of the crowd. Then we start dancing, badly, essentially doing a contemporary version of "the twist." Occasionally, I hold onto her hand and spin her around, or she wraps her arms around my neck and pushes her hips into mine, but we're both drunk and clumsy and I can't help but laugh at how uncoordinated we are. I should be embarrassed, but I don't care—I'm just happy to be with her again. She actually knows the lyrics to the song and she occasionally lip-syncs them with her eyes closed. It's cute.

When the song ends, she tells me she wants to go outside for a cigarette. We part the masses and go downstairs onto the street and then she leads me to a fire escape at the rear of the building. We climb halfway up the stairs and my knees ache and then we sit on the steps. The brick wall behind us is decorated in colourful graffiti and it shields us from the wind and everything is calm.

"I didn't know you *actually* smoked," she says as I hand her a cigarette from my pack.

"I don't, really. Only when I drink."

"Me too. Probably not a good idea to get addicted, what with the lung cancer and all."

"Yeah. It's weird. Nicotine's never really done it for me. I can smoke an entire pack in one night and never get another craving."

We both exhale and stare out into the night.

"So, let's talk about this whole law school thing," she says. "What if it doesn't pan out? Are you gonna stay in Toronto? Get a job here? Or keep studying journalism?"

"I don't know. My lease is month to month, so I can leave anytime I want, but I don't know where else I'd go. I'm kinda tired of moving around all the time, y'know? I'd like to make it work here, but it's so expensive. . . . I don't know. What about you?"

"Well, our band is recording right now, so I'm hoping we can finish by the end of the summer so we can go on tour in the fall. Nothing fancy, just around Canada. It's pretty hard to turn it into an actual career, though. I mean, everybody can just download your stuff for free."

"Yeah, but they'll still pay to see you live. And buy your shirts. I'll buy a shirt."

She smiles. "I can get you a shirt."

"Cool. I'm a medium."

"But I don't think live shows and t-shirts will pay for the van and the studio costs and all that, y'know? Don't get me wrong, I don't really care about the money, but still, I have to pay my rent *somehow*."

"I hear ya."

She exhales slowly and the smoke dissipates into the midnight air. "Music used to mean more to people, y'know? Vinyl records were really, really big." She holds out her hands vertically about a foot away from each other. "You took it home, you read the liner notes. It was art. They were valuable. People would go from store to store looking for that one rare B-side. Then they came out with tapes and CDs and the music got a little smaller and smaller. Now it's on MP3 files . . . what is that? You can't even see that. And you can download a whole record in, like, thirty seconds flat. All for free. It's the one thing in life people expect to get for free. I dunno. Maybe I'm wasting my time. I'm starting to think I should just go back to school—like you."

She's right of course. Music doesn't mean anything to me anymore. I guess I was born in the wrong decade. I love old blues songs from the forties and fifties, rock n' roll from the sixties and seventies, punk rock from the eighties, grunge and alternative from the nineties, but what is there now? Maybe I'm just bitter because I spent almost ten years—ten!—learning how to play the guitar only to realize it didn't make me special at all. Almost everybody I know can play the guitar to some extent. Guitarists are a dime a dozen. Being able to write songs and play them live and jam with other musicians to create something original—*that's* what makes you special.

So, should I tell Natalie to be idealistic and follow her dreams, or suggest she pursue a more stable career path? Part of me wishes I had spent those ten years studying to become a doctor or a professor or an accountant, but where's the fun in that? And, honestly, who am I to be giving anyone advice?

"You'll do fine," I say. "You're a really good singer."

"Thanks." She smiles and pauses to take another puff from her cigarette. "Again, I don't care about the money. I'm just sayin'."

"I know."

"Somebody told me you play guitar? It might've been Amber. Whoever it was, they said you were really good."

"I was okay. I don't really play anymore though."

"Why'd you stop?"

I shrug my shoulders. "Ah, I broke a string on my acoustic a while back and I just, y'know, never got around to fixing it."

She glares at me, baffled.

"That's it? You need a *string*?"

"It's a real pain in the ass to change those!"

She tilts her head back and laughs and then flashes me that signature smile. "I'll buy you the strings, Ethan. It'll take two minutes."

"Nah, I wouldn't remember how to play anyway."

"Why, how long has it been?"

"I don't know. . . ."

"C'mon, tell me!"

"Um . . . maybe a year or two?"

"Jesus. Are you serious? A year? Well, that settles it. I'm getting you a pack of strings next time I'm out."

I laugh and think nothing of it. "Okay. Deal."

There's a long pause. We breathe in our cigarettes and continue sitting there in silence until she says, "You don't remember calling me a couple nights ago, do you?"

"What?"

"You called me really late. I think it was on Thursday night? At like, 2AM. You don't remember this?"

"No. I don't remember anything."

"You were really drunk."

"That . . . doesn't sound like me. What'd we talk about?"

"Lots of things. We spoke for a good twenty minutes or so."

"Oh, shit."

"No, don't worry! It was fine. But I hope you feel better."

I feel my heart tighten inside my chest, and so I try to shift the blame elsewhere. "I guess I drank too much that night. It's hard to keep up with Jeff and those guys, y'know? Sometimes they really go all out."

"Hmm . . . You ever think about getting new friends?"

"What, ditch the guys? No way—"

"I didn't mean it like that, but—"

"No way. I couldn't."

"I just meant that *maybe* it would be better if you didn't hang around people who were drunk and high all the time, that's all."

"Look, I know they can seem like assholes, but they've been really loyal . . . like, no matter how badly I screw up, they always just laugh it off and invite me over the next weekend. So no . . . I couldn't ditch them like that."

"Hmm. . . . Well, anyway, I hope you feel better."

EIGHTEEN

An hour later we're back inside Sneaky Dee's and Natalie says she wants to do a shot of tequila with me. I explain that tequila is my Achilles' heel and that even a whiff of the agave plant will twist my stomach into knots, and then I tell her about the last time I drank a bottle of Jose Cuervo and how I blacked out and woke up hours later on someone else's bed in an apartment on another floor. She laughs, thinking I'm joking, but I'm not. That actually happened. I accidentally walked into the wrong room and slept there for several hours. She orders us two shots anyway, saying she'll drink mine if I can't handle it.

"Alright, but you better clear me a path to the bathroom," I tell her.

"Why?"

"Because this stuff will make me puke until I die."

She grins. "Well, you've had a good run."

I'm standing at the bar with my arm around Natalie's waist while the bartender pours us two shots. We have the lemon wedges and the salt shaker ready to go when all of a sudden an older man in a black blazer sidles up next to her and starts explaining in great detail how to do the shot: how to prepare the salt between her thumb and forefinger, when to lick it, when to drink it, and when to bite down on the lemon. The nerve of this prick! I have my arm around her and he starts hitting on her right in front of me? He looks to be over forty years old. How does he know I'm not her boyfriend? Maybe he doesn't see me as a threat, or he doesn't think a pretty girl like her could possibly be with a guy like me, but either way, it's insulting.

I can't hear what he's saying because he's whispering into her ear, but Natalie listens and nods and laughs periodically. It's hard to tell if she's merely humouring him or if she's genuinely interested; admittedly, he's better-dressed, better-looking and probably more financially secure than I am. They keep talking and ignoring me for what seems like two or three minutes while I stand there awkwardly like a third wheel. I gradually feel my blood pressure begin to rise and I lose patience. Maybe it's the alcohol. Or the cocaine. Or both. I don't think it's in Natalie's nature to tell somebody to fuck off, but it sure as hell is in mine.

"Hey! Why don't you fuck off?" I yell at him.

That got his attention. He breaks his trance with Natalie and looks over at me. "What?"

"You heard me. Fuck off. Right now."

"Ethan? What're you doing? It's okay," Natalie says, calmly putting her hand on my arm.

"No, it's not okay!" I shout. "I'm standing right here and he starts hitting on you? He's like, forty years old! You're forty years old, asshole! What, can't get someone your own age? Gotta hit on college girls, you fucking loser?"

The man glares at me with seething eyes as he slowly steps around Natalie and moves toward me until our faces are mere inches apart. Luckily, I'm slightly taller than he is. I stare back at him and grit my teeth and then clench my right hand into a fist, waiting for him to either throw a punch or walk away. I refuse to walk away. Not with everybody watching. I'd rather get the shit kicked out of me than look like a coward. The tension reaches a boiling point. In the corner of my eye, I see two members of the security staff monitoring the situation; if I try to hit him, they'll immediately wrestle me to the ground and drag me out of the club, but not before I catch him with a good shot or two.

I hold my breath. He stands perfectly still with his lip curled. Then he glances to his left and notices the bouncers watching us closely; with a smirk on his face, he slowly raises his open palms in a placating gesture before calmly stepping away to the side. Then, as he's walking past me, he rams his shoulder into my upper arm. The hit is jarring, but I stand my ground and stare straight ahead. "You better watch your fucking mouth," he mutters. "Something's gonna happen to you." I keep looking forward until he disappears through the exit and the security staff gradually disperse.

"What the hell was that?" Natalie snaps.

"That guy was an asshole! How'd he know I wasn't your boyfriend?"

"He was just talking, Ethan. I could've handled it. You didn't have to pick a fight."

"If I didn't say anything, he never would've left!"

At that moment somebody taps me on the shoulder; I expect to turn around and see another bouncer, but instead it's a skinny guy with long hair and a shaggy beard.

"I saw all of that," the stranger tells me. "And I just wanted to say I would've done the exact same thing."

"Hey, thanks, man."

"He can't come on to her like that. Not right in front of you. That's not cool."

"I know! See? This guy gets it."

I return my attention to Natalie only to find yet another man flirting with her. This one is younger and clean-cut and he has a smug, condescending grin on his face. "What's this guy's problem?" he asks her as he drapes his arm across her shoulders. "Little overprotective, huh?"

I have no patience left and I'm still chock-full of adrenaline from the last encounter, so I immediately cock my fist and say, "Get the fuck outta here before I beat the shit outta you!"

"Whoa. Relax, buddy. I'm leaving." He smiles at me through his teeth and then struts back to his circle of friends where they giggle and sneer at me.

In the midst of all the animosity, I realize I forgot to drink my tequila. "Cheers," I say to no one in particular while holding up the glass by the rim. Then I toss back the shot without using the salt or the lemon and the tequila burns my mouth and sinuses and makes my innards feel nauseous from the scent. I tighten my eyes and scrunch my face, worrying I might vomit, but the feeling quickly subsides.

Natalie stands there glaring at me with her arms crossed. "Hey, you know that guy you just threatened? His name's Dylan. I work with him."

Now I feel like I'm going to be sick again.

"Aw, shit, Natalie. I didn't know. . . ."

"I'm going out for a smoke," she mutters. Then she departs through the crowd and walks down the stairs without me. As I'm watching her go, one of the bouncers approaches me from the side and lightly taps me on the upper arm. "Alright, man, I think it's time to go," he says as he begins to usher me toward the exit.

"Get your fuckin' hands off me," I groan. "I'm leaving."

The bouncer escorts me down the stairs and pushes me through the doorway at the bottom where I find Natalie standing outside the entrance with her arms still crossed and a cigarette hanging between her two fingers.

"Hey, I'm sorry," I tell her. "I don't know what got into me. I blame the tequila, really. We never should've ordered that."

"You were being a *bit* of an asshole. . . ."

"I know."

We stand there in silence for a moment before Natalie sighs and puts out her cigarette and then says, "Look, Ethan, I think I'm gonna go home."

"Natalie, come on—"

"You should probably call it a night too. I've had a long day and I think we both drank way too much."

"Okay, fine, but let's at least split a cab? My sense of direction is kinda messed up right now. . . . I don't know how to get home from here."

She seems distracted, like she's not really listening to me. Then she closely examines my face and points at me and says, solemnly, "You have some white stuff on your nose."

I hurriedly wipe at my nostrils and examine my fingertips to find small remnants of cocaine. Was it there the whole time? When I look up again, she's already walking in the opposite direction. I follow behind her until we're both standing alone on the street corner.

"On Thursday night, when you called, do you remember what we talked about?" she asks. "You told me about this girl Rachael. Remember that?"

"No. I don't remember anything."

"You said you two were close. For, like, ten years." She takes a long, deep breath before continuing. "And then you told me that she died . . . and you still weren't over it."

My face goes pale and I remain silent.

"So I worry about you when you get like this."

"Look . . . I'm sorry about tonight. I don't know where that came from. I, uh . . ."

My voice trails off.

"You don't have to explain anything to me, Ethan."

"Let me make it up to you, okay? Don't leave. We can go somewhere and talk."

She shakes her head. "I'm sorry. I gotta go."

I stand frozen on the corner while she turns away from me and crosses the street. No hugs, no handshakes or goodbyes. A streetcar is waiting for her on the other side, and by the time I decide to chase after her I lose her in the swarm of oncoming passengers. As the car departs, I slump down on the curb and lower my head between my knees and close my eyes.

NINETEEN

I'm angry. So angry I want to scream. Angry at the forty-year-old man, that smug co-worker friend Dylan, and at the world in general. Incensed, I send Natalie a barrage of drunken text messages berating her for leaving me lost in the middle of downtown Toronto. She doesn't reply. That's the part that gets me the most: she doesn't care. Doesn't care if I'm upset or if I don't make it home or if we never speak again. All it would take is a one-word response—just one word!—to let me know she actually gives a shit and then I'd apologize immediately. But, deep down, I know I'm not actually angry at her. She did nothing wrong. I'm furious with myself for getting blackout drunk on a Thursday night and calling her at two o'clock in the morning and telling her about Rachael.

The appropriate thing to do would be to go home. Sleep it off. Sober up and try to make amends in the morning. I know this. But I also know I'll never be able to fall asleep: my heart will pound and my mind will race and the pain in my chest will become excruciating. I'll spend the night recounting every word, every moment, trying to determine where it went wrong and what it means and how to explain myself to her in the future.

No. I can't go home yet. Not like this.

I retrieve my phone and dial Andre's number. Andre sells drugs. Real drugs—not just marijuana and mushrooms. I first met him a few months ago outside a bar on Bloor Street; I was asking around for some cocaine and somebody pointed me in his direction. He was surprisingly upfront about what he sold—I guess he could tell I wasn't a cop. That, or he was brazenly reckless, but reckless dealers usually don't stay in business for very long. He gave me his number and told me to call if I ever needed anything else. I've called him a few times since. We have a standard rendezvous point in an alleyway where we make the exchange and then quickly part ways—I don't know anything else about him aside from his name and number.

"Andre. It's Reid."

"Hey, what's up, man? Lookin' for something?"

"Yeah. I've had a pretty rough night."

"Shit, sorry to hear that! I can't really leave my place right now though 'cause I've got some people over. . . . Why don't you stop by here?"

"Really? You sure?"

"Yeah, man, it's cool."

Andre gives me the address to his apartment and, unsurprisingly, it's only about a block away from where we usually meet. He buzzes me in and I have to take the stairs because the building is old and there's no elevator. When I knock on his door, I can hear loud rock music playing on the other side followed by the sound of footsteps.

The door opens. "Come on in!" Andre says.

His apartment is very spacious, probably a three-bedroom, but it feels bare and empty due to the plain, cream-coloured walls. There's little in the way of furniture aside from a couch, a coffee table and a big flat screen television in the living room. Four of Andre's friends are busy crushing hash in a coffee grinder in the kitchen and they completely ignore me. I collapse onto the couch as Andre grabs a rolling desk chair from the corner of the room and pulls it forward to sit down.

"Hey man, good to see ya," he says. "You hungry at all? Want a candy bar? We're eating Coffee Crisp!"

"Sure, I'll take one."

He passes me a bowl of bite-sized chocolate bars that look as if they've been sitting there since last Halloween. I take two and unwrap them while he's talking. "Had a shitty night, huh?" he asks.

"Yeah."

"Ah, sorry to hear that. I've got something cool for you though." He rises from his chair and disappears into the hallway for a moment and then returns with a thin orange bottle. "My roommate just had his wisdom teeth pulled out and they gave him a bunch of codeine. There's still half a bottle left. You can have it. They load it up with caffeine and some other shit, but you can extract all that with some warm water and a coffee filter. Then you leave it in the fridge for a while and—"

"I know. I've done it before. Thanks, man."

The directions on the label read TAKE 1–2 TABLETS EVERY 3–5 HOURS WHEN NECESSARY FOR PAIN. There's also a red sticker warning about the dangers of combining it with alcohol or operating heavy machinery. I open the bottle and pop a pill into my mouth, swallow, and then pocket the rest.

"So, what else are you looking for?"

"Coke. I had some tonight and now I want more."

"Alright, man! It'll run you at least forty bucks, though, depending on how much you want."

"I don't need much."

"Cool." Andre leaves the room and returns a minute later with a square piece of paper folded inward at the corners. I hand him the money and he counts it as I get up to leave. On my way out, he says, "By the way, be careful with that codeine shit! I read somewhere that, over the long term, it'll totally fuck up your dick."

I scoff. "I don't think I'll be needing *that* tonight."

"Bullshit! I've seen you! You're a ladies man! Why don't you go say hi to Vanessa? She'll cheer you up, ya mope!"

I halfheartedly smile and then give him a quick nod before exiting through the doorway and down the stairs and back out into the darkness.

TWENTY

Vanessa is a masseuse who stays open past midnight in case somebody desperately needs a massage at 2AM. That's the official story anyway. In actuality, she moonlights as a prostitute. Andre introduced me to her one night when I was loaded and I've met up with her two or three times since. Vanessa often talks about going to law school, so we do have that in common. One time, we spent over half an hour discussing the admissions test and I even offered to help her study for it. Protocol says you have to book appointments in advance, but tonight I can't call ahead because I don't have her phone number. Still, I figure it's worth a shot—she knows who I am by now. And I could really use the company. The streets are dead quiet and the only sound I hear is the echo of my own footsteps.

Twenty minutes later I find myself standing in front of her massage parlour where there's a conspicuous guard dressed in black monitoring the door. Unlike the short, round bouncer who kicked me out of Lee's Palace, this guy is an absolute giant; he wears a black skullcap and has long hair like a pro wrestler.

"Hey. I'm here to see Vanessa."

"One second." He pulls out a phone and pushes the redial button. "Is she expecting you?"

"No. But she knows me."

"Your name?"

"Reid."

He nods and waits for the person on the other end of the line to answer. "Hey. A guy named Reid here to see you? Uh huh. Yeah. Okay." He closes the phone.

"Can I go in?"

"No. She's not expecting you."

"You told her it was me?"

"Yeah, I told her it was you."

"And she's still not gonna let me in?"

"No. You gotta call beforehand."

"I left her business card at home."

"Well, call ahead next time. Now keep walking."

Nothing is going my way tonight—not with Natalie, not with Caitlyn, not with anything. It's getting colder outside and I'm still a long way from home. Vanessa is my last refuge.

"Let me talk to her. Can I use your phone?"

"No. You have to leave, man."

"It'll only take a second."

"No."

"Why not?"

"Because I told you to fuck off."

"Come on, just lemme talk to her. . . ."

I slowly reach for his phone, which he interprets as a threat, and so he shoves me in the chest with his right hand. The force catches by surprise and knocks me off balance; I fall backwards to the ground and my head smacks against the pavement. For a moment I lie motionless on the sidewalk with the whole city spinning around me. Then I touch the back of my skull and feel a small amount of blood oozing through my hair. While still lying flat, I pull my hip flask out of my pocket and take a big mouthful of gin. When I try to stand up again, my legs wobble like broken stilts. City life is hard on the knees.

"Christ, man," I say. "Relax!"

"I'm not babysitting you all night. Get the fuck outta here."

"Wait. I'll go. I just have one more question."

"What."

"Do you know where that after-hours club is? The one on Queen? I've been there before, but I don't remember the street number."

"Can't tell you."

"Why not?"

"You might be a cop."

"Do I *look* like a cop?"

"Even if it's only a small chance, it's not worth the risk."

"I swear I'm not a cop. Just tell me!"

"Not worth it."

I hold up my hip flask. "I'll give you some gin?"

"No."

"Ah, you're fuckin' useless."

With that, I awkwardly stumble away. The cut on the back of my head is bleeding slightly, so I rub a little gin on it to prevent an infection, but that only worsens the burning. I continue walking for a full city block before I suddenly realize that Andre would have Vanessa's phone number. I can just get it from him. I call Andre and he happily gives me her number which I promptly program into my phone; I should've made note of it before, but for some odd reason I didn't like the idea of having a prostitute on my contact list.

I dial Vanessa's number and wait for her to answer. I have to call twice because she screens her calls.

"Hello?"

"Hey. This is Ethan."

"Oh, hey, how's it going?" she says. She seems to be feigning recognition—I can tell because it's something I do all the time. "Are you looking to make an appointment?"

"No. Actually, I was trying to get in there a few minutes ago, but your stupid doorman manhandled me." I notice I'm slurring my speech and I hope she can't tell. "He pushed me around and totally knocked me over and now I'm bleeding. You should really do something about that guy."

"Oh, honey, I'm sorry about that. Why didn't you call me earlier?"

"Well, I forgot to bring your business card and that asshole wouldn't let me talk to you. I've never had a problem getting in on short notice before. I just don't think it's fair, y'know? I shouldn't be treated like that. I mean, I've been a good customer and—"

"I know you have, hun." Again, I don't think she actually remembers who I am. "But we've been having some problems with security lately, so the best way is to just call ahead. That way, this kind of thing doesn't happen. Why don't you come by tomorrow?"

"After tonight, I don't think I ever wanna come back."

"Well, I don't think that's really fair to *me*."

"You should've remembered my name! I was gonna help you get into law school, remember? We talked about it for, like, an hour!" It's then I realize I'm in the midst of a heated argument with a prostitute; I press the phone against my chest and lower my head, taking a moment to ponder how it all came to this. "I was gonna spend a lot of money in there tonight."

"How?" she asks condescendingly. "There's a standard rate."

"I know, but I . . . I was gonna leave a tip—or something. Anyway, I think I'm just gonna take my money elsewhere from now on. So, goodbye, Vanessa. Good luck with law school."

I hang up the phone and take another shot from my flask. I feel staggeringly drunk. My internal compass is gone, my eyesight is blurry and dizzy, and balance is eluding me. It's like being on auto-pilot: you can still walk and talk, but your mind is no longer in control. It follows you along like a spectator, watching you move and speak and act in the third-person. Before I know it, I've walked for more than half an hour and have no idea where I am. Taxis speed past me in both directions and I need to hail one, but, opening my wallet, I see I only have a ten-dollar bill and some pocket change left—not nearly enough to make it home. Spotting a park bench, I take off my jacket and roll it up into a ball and tuck it underneath my head like a pillow. Even though I'm in the middle of a bustling city, surrounded by millions of people, I can't help but feel utterly alone.

TWENTY-ONE

Rachael never criticized me for drinking. Even though she had seen me "drink my weight in alcohol" on more than one occasion, she always accepted it for what it was. Maybe she saw it as a passing phase and nothing more, but she never raised the topic in conversation.

Whenever the two of us drank together, I was always happy and content to stay indoors. I remember sitting cross-legged on the carpet and playing beer caps. I remember curling up on the couch and laughing hysterically at the British version of *The Office*. I remember passing an acoustic guitar back and forth and showing each other different songs and chord progressions. I remember her teaching me how to play a major scale on the piano by crossing the thumb underneath the fingers. I remember taking silly black-and-white photos with my webcam. I remember her convincing me to try a gin-and-tonic for the first time and how much I hated it. I remember conversations that lasted until three o'clock in the morning, long after everyone else had fallen sleep. In retrospect, when she was around, I didn't even need the alcohol.

I'm lying on a park bench and staring up at a few pale stars in the night sky. It's quiet here, but I know I'm not going to fall asleep. Not ready to pass out just yet. I stand up and gather my jacket and then continue to stroll aimlessly through the side streets, eventually passing a small church courtyard in the midst of a residential area. Three girls in their early twenties dressed like goth-hippies are crouching on the grass beside a pile of rocks and bricks and stones. They notice me as I amble past and one of them calls out, "Hey, do you wanna help us build our cathedral?"

Curious as to what that means, I approach them. "What cathedral?"

"*Our* cathedral." She points at the rocks on the ground and I realize they're positioned like Lego blocks to create a miniature model of the old church that stands behind us.

"I don't know if I'd be much help. I gotta confess . . . I'm pretty high right now."

"Why, what're you on?" another girl asks.

"Mostly booze, a little codeine, some . . . Coffee Crisp."

A brief hush falls over the girls, but they're not judgmental. They casually accept my drug use for what it is.

"So what's your name?" the first girl asks. She wears thick black eyeliner and her hair is dyed dark purple, which matches well with her gloves, piercings and tattoos.

"I'm Ethan."

"No, no, no!" she says. "That's your *Christian* name! It was given to you before you were born by people who knew nothing about you. What's your *real* name?"

"What do you mean?"

"Well, my name is Swan. This here is Dive and her name is Hype. Your name should reflect your *true* self. Who you are on the inside, regardless of race or religion or what society thinks of you. It isn't given to you. You pick it. Anything you want."

"Oh. Okay. So why 'Swan'?"

"I used to be really into Greek mythology, right? And one time I read this story about how Zeus used the form of a swan to seduce and rape Leda. From that point on, I decided to go by Swan."

"How could a swan rape someone?" I wonder aloud.

They ignore my question. "I chose Dive because it's the name of my favourite song," says the second girl.

"I see. And Hype?" I ask.

"She's a hypersomniac," says Swan. "It means she sleeps, like, twelve hours a day." I glance over at Hype and she yawns on cue. "But enough about us! Come on! What's your name?"

I consider the question a moment, trying to think of a single word that defines my true self, my entire being, my ultimate purpose on this earth. But nothing comes to mind.

"I don't know."

"Don't worry. You'll know it. Eventually," Swan assures me. Then she squats down and continues working on the model cathedral. "We're not from around here, you know."

"We're from the West Coast," says Dive. "We travelled across the whole country just to be here." Then she tells me about their long trip and how they rode the rails all the way from British Columbia, stopping at various towns and making money by busking and selling jewelry they made themselves. It must be nice to have that kind of freedom, to be able to make a living on the road. I ask them why they're in Toronto and they tell me they're here for a spoken word festival.

"Spoken word?"

"It's poetry," says Swan. "Lyrical freestyle."

"I've never heard of it before."

All three gasp in disbelief. Then Hype stands up suddenly and launches into a verbal stream of consciousness, enunciating each syllable with a rhythm and a flow as if it were set to music: "You must be blind, what will it take you to see? This confusion, collusion, and conformity? Like a celebrity on the screen surrounded by whores, with a cold sore mouth and an unnamed source. Delusion, contusion, that's affecting my brain. An appetite, a hunger, that could never be tamed. What can I do, to make you believe—"

"Alright, I get it," I interrupt. My mind is too murky to follow along and the multi-syllabic words hurt my brain.

She ignores me and continues: "—the stress in this mess is only somewhat conceived, by a gov'ment that's supposed to comply to the need—"

"Aw man, you gotta stop!"

"—of the people they ignore to a narrow degree, as a threat to their nest but what we can achieve, if the limit is to live it in the realm—of possibility."

Having finished her poem, she stares at me a moment, the two of us blinking at each other in unison. Then she quietly slumps down with her legs crossed and calmly carries on with the construction of the model cathedral.

"So yeah, that's spoken word," says Swan.

"Neat," I reply.

"You should come see us tomorrow night," says Dive. "We're all performing at this place in Kensington Market. It's us and, like, eight other people. They're all really good too."

"I would, but I've . . . uh . . . got a lot of stuff to do."

The girls look disappointed, and a long pause ensues. Then Swan says ominously, "You can't keep running like this, Ethan. You can't."

"What do you mean?"

"You're running! From us. From the truth. From your *dark past*. From everything!"

"What makes you think I have a *dark past*?"

"Oh, come on! It's so obvious. Only someone who's trying to punish himself would get high on drugs and then stumble into a church at two o'clock in the morning."

"You called me over!"

"Because you need to be saved!"

"From what?"

"From yourself. From society. From that *dark past* of yours. You don't even know your real name!"

"I don't have a dark past!"

Swan glares at me, skeptically. "Who are you trying to convince, huh? Us? Or you?"

"Look! He's blushing!" says Dive.

Hype begins to chuckle under her breath.

"Alright! Fine! Maybe I do have a dark past! But . . . fucking *poetry* isn't gonna change that."

"Did he just say 'butt-fucking poetry'?" Dive asks.

"No, I meant—"

"Spoken word," Swan corrects me. "It's butt-fucking spoken word. And it'll change your life, if you let it." Approaching me, she runs her fingers through my hair and gently brushes her hand down the side of my cheek, all while staring straight into my eyes as if she's trying to put me into a trance. "Put aside the past, Ethan. And come see us tomorrow night. In Kensington Market. Five-dollar cover. Three-dollar beer. Domestic only."

TWENTY-TWO

My phone vibrates. It's Doc calling to inform me they're on their way to the after-hours club. It doesn't have a name, but we call it the "White Room" on account of the colour of the walls and the prevalence of cocaine. He reminds me of the address and I tell him I'll meet him there in ten minutes. Then I hang up the phone and ask the three girls if they know how to get back to Queen Street and they point me in the right direction. I give them my thanks and wish them good luck with the spoken word festival.

"You better come tomorrow!" Swan calls out to me. "Remember, you promised!"

"I will!" I answer as I sprint across the road.

"It's your *only hope!*" she warns, stressing the last two words like a ghost in a Charles Dickens novel.

You would never find the White Room unless you knew precisely where to look. There are no lights, no signs, no noise. Nothing but an inconspicuous white door and a street number above the frame. Inside, however, is a different story: you can typically find about a hundred people smoking cigarettes, shooting pool and listening to live bands perform next to a fully staffed bar serving every kind of alcohol for a reasonable price until six o'clock in the morning. During prohibition, they would've called this place a speakeasy or a blind tiger and it would've been just as illegal.

Before going inside, I sneak into a deserted alleyway around the side of the building and find an alcove to cower in. Then I unwrap the folded paper I bought from Andre to reveal a small mound of cocaine. I reach into my wallet and roll up my ten-dollar bill and use it to snort the drug into my nasal cavity. The instant euphoria briefly returns and I exhale in relief, but the emptiness is still there, stewing in the pit of my chest. I desperately inhale more of it in an attempt to recapture the exhilaration I felt earlier, accidentally spilling some of the drug all over my nose and upper lip. In frustration, I crumple up the paper and throw it against the wall and a small flurry of dust evaporates into the air. What a waste of money.

I wipe my nose and mouth and return to the front of the building and tap on the door three times. Within seconds, I'm swiftly ushered inside by a tall man in black and led through several empty rooms until I'm brought to a desk where a young woman is collecting a cover fee. I pay her using the same ten-dollar bill before walking inside.

Behind the curtain there are two pool tables, a smoking room and a long lineup of people waiting to use the bathroom, but the real party is on the second floor where a punk band is belting out a raucous version of "Something I Learned Today" by Hüsker Dü. A few stoners bob their heads in front of the stage while the rest of the patrons lounge on the couches and chairs that line the walls, which are decorated with thick purple drapes hung from the ceiling. You would never know it was an illegal bar from the inside: the security, the waitresses, the bartenders and the decor all bear resemblance to every other law-abiding establishment in the city. The only difference is, in here, we can drink and smoke and take drugs until sunrise.

I meander past the bar through a mob of people until I find Doc and Scott relaxing on one of the couches with their legs outstretched. They're clearly drunk; when I pull up a chair, they can only muster a halfhearted greeting and for some reason their hair is wet.

"Oh, man, you missed out!" Doc exclaims. "We went to this swimming pool at Christie Pits and it was awesome. Me, Scott, and like thirty other people hopped the fence and swam in our undies! There's a huge water slide, a bunch of diving boards, and a lot of girls went topless. . . . It was awesome."

"I'm going back there every weekend," Scott mutters.

So while I was busy arguing with a prostitute and listening to spoken word poetry, I could have been jumping down a giant water slide and staring at half-naked women. Well done, Reid.

"What happened to Craig and Nikki?" I ask.

"Nikki had to go home early for some reason and Craig left the bar with some blonde chick," says Doc.

"She was fairly attractive," Scott tells me. "And she had big cans. But yeah, I don't think I can stay out much longer. I gotta go to job tomorrow."

"What time do you have to 'go to job'?"

"I gotta leave my place at, like, eight-thirty."

"Man, that's in six hours! You'll never make it."

"You . . . shut your mouth. I'll make it easy."

"C'mon, Scott!" says Doc. "Don't be such a goddamn pussy. Stick around for another couple hours."

"Okay," he replies.

After a few more minutes of lazing on the couch, Doc grows impatient and starts surveying the room. "Man, there are some decent-looking girls in here. We should be hitting on them."

"You really shouldn't," Scott replies. "Your genitals are riddled with diseases."

"One disease!" he shouts, holding up an index finger. Then he turns to me and says, "Craig texted me earlier and said his new lady-friend has a couple roommates. He's gonna try to get them to invite us over . . . so, basically, he's our last hope for getting laid tonight."

"No!" Scott objects. "He's not our last hope! He's not *Star Wars*! I still have a shot. I just need another drink. Then I'll go find a girl with low self-esteem."

"Dude, I can't buy another beer," Doc says. "I don't have any burn money left and there's no ATM. But look! Some girls left their drinks. Let's just take them."

On the table in front of us there are two yellow cocktails served in curvy glasses with little plastic umbrellas and rims garnished with maraschino cherries.

"No way," Scott says. "What are they?"

"I think they're called 'bee stings,'" I tell him. I raise one of the glasses to my nose and it smells like honey. "Yup. Definitely a bee sting."

"I'm sure they taste good," Doc says.

"Well, I'm not drinking those," Scott declares.

"Hey!" Doc yells, slamming his fist onto the table. "Are we gonna drink these bee stings . . . or are we gonna be *faggots*?"

Long pause.

"Fine, I'll drink it," Scott replies.

"Dude! You shouldn't say that," I warn Doc.

"What, 'faggot'?" he repeats loudly. As expected, people in the immediate area take notice and frown. "I can say anything I want all the time!"

"You're gonna offend someone!"

"Whatever, man! Why should I give a shit if they take it the wrong way? I meant it, like, 'stop being an annoying faggot.' Not the homophobic way."

"But some people might not make that distinction!"

"Hey! I support gay rights, dude! What do I care if two consenting adults wanna engage in hot, man-on-man action? I'm using the word in a different context in order to *change* the definition. I call everybody faggots! I told my sister she was being a faggot yesterday! Those people should be *thanking* me."

"Just shut the fuck up and drink your bee sting!"

The two of them sip feverishly on the straws of their stolen cocktails and within a minute the glasses are completely dry.

"Well, that was delicious," says Scott.

Unsatisfied, Doc mutters, "I'm still kinda thirsty though."

"Well, I'm gonna go buy another gin-and-tonic," I tell them. Thankfully, I still have enough coins on me for one last drink. Doc follows me to the bar where we stand in line behind several other people. One of them looks a lot like the bouncer from Vanessa's parlour; I lower my head and turn away to make sure he doesn't see me. The last thing I need is another confrontation with that goon. Fortunately, he buys a drink and immediately leaves through the stairwell. We order our drinks and the bartender—a very attractive girl with long blue hair—hands us a

gin-and-tonic and a bottle of beer. I give her my change while
Doc empties out his pockets, trying to pay with something other
than money.

"All I have are these subway tokens. . . . Oh! And an individual pack of crackers. They're salted." To my surprise, she actually
accepts the tokens as payment. Apparently she rides the subway
quite often. "Keep the *change*," he tells her, pronouncing the word
as though it rhymes with "dawn."

Doc and I take our drinks to the front of the stage and watch
the band play a paint-by-numbers punk set including all of the
classics from Black Flag, The Sex Pistols and the first record by
The Clash. As we stand there bobbing our heads to the music, I
notice a girl making eye contact with me. She has straight black
bangs, dark eyes and massive breasts—obviously, she's way out of
my league. Throughout the night I watch several other men try
to make a pass at her, but not one of them is even remotely successful; she bats them away like she's swatting at flies.
Occasionally, when we're all jumping around to the chorus, she
intentionally bumps into me and then leans up against me, as if
she wants to say something, but she never does. Maybe she's teasing me.

When the band hits the cymbals on their final song, we
applaud and cheer and whistle as they vacate the stage. The girl
with the dark eyes finally locks onto me and advances. I feel Doc
shove me forward from behind, and then he scurries away like a
cockroach in daylight and it's only me and her. She speaks first.

"Hey. I like you. You're polite . . . unlike some of the other
boys in here." Her accent is Eastern European and she reminds me
of a James Bond villain. "I have a surprise for you," she whispers,
holding out her hand to reveal a small yellow capsule.

"Whoa. What's that?"

"MDMA. It'll make you feel amazing."

"You're not gonna take advantage of me, are you? 'Cause I'm
feeling pretty vulnerable right now."

She laughs. "If you don't want it, I'll keep it for myself." She
slowly brings the pill to her lips and I grab her wrist to stop her
from putting it in her mouth.

"Wait. I'll try it. But . . . just don't let me pass out here."

"I won't."

I place the capsule on my tongue and chase it with gin. I've tried ecstasy before, but this is supposedly more potent. Every time I experiment with a new drug I feel a deep fear of the unknown—the fear that I might have an allergic reaction or hallucinate or lose control of myself and run around naked screaming "Attica! Attica!" In this case, my fear is amplified because this girl is a stranger; for all I know, she could have given me a roofie. Maybe she'll steal my wallet. Or my kidney. If I wake up tomorrow in a bathtub full of ice with a big scar across my back, I'm going to be really pissed off.

"Wait until it settles in," she tells me. "You'll feel amazing."

"What's your name?" I ask.

"Sofia."

"Ethan. Where are you from?"

"Russia. Armenia, to be exact. Do you like Armenian girls?"

"You're the first one I've met, but you seem pretty nice."

Whenever I meet someone from Russia, I immediately ask them about the Cold War, the Summit Series and *Rocky IV*, but with Sofia I refrain.

"I love Canadian boys. You're so nice." She grabs me by the wrist and scratches me with her fingernails, digging deep into the skin, so deep she almost draws blood. "Do you feel it yet?"

"I'm starting to get a little tingly."

"Good," she says.

Suddenly, I hear Doc whistling and catcalling at me from across the room. I figure he's teasing me, but when I turn around I see him standing at a table with four other people and he's motioning for us to join them. Sofia and I approach the group and he introduces us to a handsome, well-dressed man in his mid-thirties named Ben who apparently works as a television producer in Los Angeles. Ben, his tall blonde girlfriend, and his two buddies are out celebrating because he recently sold a new reality show to a major cable network. In his right hand he holds a ziplock bag full of white powder which he periodically offers to the table, bringing it directly to our noses with a tiny metal scoop. We all partake, including Sofia.

"I grew up here, but I moved out to L.A. like, ten years ago," Ben tells us. "Eventually, I'd like to get into movies, but you gotta start somewhere, right? The fact of the matter is, reality shows are the most lucrative thing in the business right now 'cause they're so cheap to produce. You don't have to pay actors, you usually don't need writers, so your production costs stay low. That's why practically every channel is jumping on it—even the artsy, high-brow ones. But it's hard to keep it fresh, you know what I mean? I mean, you can always . . ."

For the next five minutes he continues to drone on about his issues with the contemporary television industry and I have no interest in what he's saying, but I nod and smile and listen polite-ly nonetheless while I wait for him to offer me another hit. I feel like a real big shot, snorting cocaine from a TV producer with Sofia hanging on my arm. I could get used to this.

"You should hear my movie idea!" Doc exclaims.

"Why, what is it?" Ben asks.

"Okay, so it's about this cop, right? He's a real live wire who plays hard and fast with the rules, but he ultimately gets the job done, y'know? I was thinking DiCaprio, or McConaughey, or maybe Diesel—any badass, really. Anyway, at the start of the movie, he's trying to bring down this big crime boss, but he's got a bunch of other *shit* going on. Like, personal issues and *shit*. And then, at the end of the movie, you find out that the bad guy he's been chasing after for the past two-and-a-half hours is actually *him*! He was hunting *himself* the whole time. . . ."

There's a long pause before Ben finally says, "Wow . . . that . . . that sounds awful."

"It's good, alright?" Doc snarls, and then with disdain he screams, "It's a good movie for people who aren't *FAGGOTS*!"

This causes a furious uproar at the table. Doc and Ben and his friends start pointing and shouting and shaking their fists at each other, arguing about the merit of Doc's movie idea, while Sofia and I remain silent. Suddenly, a bouncer at the far side of the room slams a door to get our attention and the music screeches to a halt. Everything goes quiet. Then he calls out, "Alright! Everybody file out through the back! The cops are out front!"

At that precise moment, of course, the MDMA kicks in. Perfect timing. I feel dizzy and light seems to stay in my eyes for longer than usual and the nerve endings in my arms and legs begin to feel warm and sensitive as they tremble. Then I drop my plastic cup on the floor and gin spills everywhere.

"Fuck!" I shout. Sofia sighs and grabs me by the hand and her grip feels different now. Very soft. As we're all shuffling through the main room, I suddenly remember Scott and run back through the crowd to find him unconscious on the couch with drool dripping from his mouth. Doc wakes him up by slapping him unnecessarily hard in the face several times and then we help him to his feet. Sofia leads us down a set of stairs into a utility room filled with stacks of empty beer cases and the concrete floor is soaking wet. There's an exit at the end of the room which takes us outside into an alleyway—the same alcove where I snorted cocaine earlier.

The four of us quietly follow the herd, careful not to alert the police on the opposite side of the building as we evacuate the area. No sign of Ben or any of his friends. They must have escaped before us. We see a police cruiser parked by the main road and manage to evade it by sneaking behind a short wooden fence through a darkened path. Once we're at a safe distance we stop to gather our bearings and catch our breath. While he's panting, Doc strikes up a conversation with Sofia.

"So . . . you're from Russia?"

"Yes. I'm Russian-Armenian."

"And what brings you to Toronto?"

"Well, when I was young, there was a lot of fighting and conflict in my country. I had to leave. It was very, very violent there. I saw some . . . unspeakable things."

"Like what?" Scott asks.

"I can't say. That's why it's unspeakable."

"Oh."

"My apartment is nearby," Sofia whispers into my ear. "Walk with me there." And then, inexplicably, she takes off her shirt. Why, I don't know—maybe she's feeling the warming effects of the MDMA too. Her bra is black and her breasts are pouring out over the top and I can't help but stare. Within seconds she is surrounded by a circle of random men, most of whom left the after-hours club alongside us. They're all hooting and hollering at her at the same time, drowning each other out. Thankfully, Sofia has no interest in any of them, so she reaches through the crowd and takes me by the hand again.

"Alright!" I shout. "Show's over! I'm walking her home."

I hear a few resentful groans and disparaging remarks as they gradually disperse, and one of them continues to follow us as we walk down the road. At the first intersection Doc hails a taxi before grabbing Scott by the neck and the belt and literally throwing him into the backseat. "I'll talk to you tomorrow," he says. Then he winks at me as if to wish me luck before closing the door and speeding off.

We continue walking in the direction of Sofia's apartment, and that stalker from the club is still following behind us. It's creepy, and we try our best to ignore him. Along the way, she says out of the blue, "Can I ask you *one* question? Are you circumcised?"

I'm not circumcised, but I'm not sure that's what she wants to hear. So I say, "Uh, which style do you prefer?"

"I don't like it when they're uncircumcised. It's not as clean, I think?"

"Oh. Good. Because I've never *been* more circumcised."

"Okay. I know I'm gonna see it anyway, but I just wanna know."

Sofia's apartment building looks new and expensive with its shiny black walls. Through the window, situated in the lobby, I can see classy leather furniture and exotic green plants. She stops me in front of the entrance by pushing her palm against my chest and then, without warning, she pulls my face toward hers and starts kissing me. Our timing is a little off—presumably because of the drugs—but we keep kissing until she laments, "You Canadian boys are so nice."

"I'm not *that* nice," I mutter.

"Hmm. I doubt that. I'm sorry, but you can't come in tonight. My roommate is sleeping and she will not allow it. But, if you call me tomorrow, I might let you take me out."

Part of me is actually relieved Sofia doesn't want to bring me upstairs. I'm probably too drunk and miserable to perform even if prompted, and when she catches a glimpse of that foreskin it's all over. Still, the thought of being with her in a nice warm bed is comforting and I don't want to be alone. "Can I use your bathroom real quick? Get a cup of coffee? Do you have a dog? I really want to meet him."

She laughs. "Not tonight."

"Well, it was worth a shot."

"Now, Ethan, let me tell you something for your own good."

"Uh oh," I mumble, predicting some forthcoming criticism.

"Listen," she says while rubbing my shoulders. "You only live once. This here . . . it's all temporary. After that, it's gone. And either you did it, or you didn't do it, so as long as you're not hurting anybody, you should really take that chance."

"So . . . you're saying you want me to sleep with you?"

She laughs again. "No! I can't tonight. I'm asking you what you *really* want to do. I mean, in the big picture."

I look down at the pavement and consider the question. What would really make me happy? Everything I've ever wanted to do seems so impossible now. Granted, I'm only twenty-four years old, but I've been in college for the last six years and I can't stay in school for the rest of my life. I don't want to be paying off student loans until I'm sixty. Sure, I would love to have a job where I could travel and see the world, but it's just not in the cards. I chose the wrong degree, plain and simple. Literature. History. Journalism. Why did I study those things? Nobody cares about those things anymore.

We have too many goddamn choices nowadays: ice cream flavours, cellphone plans, hair care products, toothpaste brands, TV channels, university courses—there are too many to choose from. With so many options, not only is it more difficult to make a decision, we're never satisfied with the decision we make because we're always wondering what the grass is like on the other side. How are you supposed to know which side is right?

"I don't know what I want to do," I tell her. "I've tried different schools, different cities, worked a bunch of shitty jobs, but nothing ever seems to stick. Honestly, I just don't think I'm good at anything."

"I didn't ask you what you were good at," she says. Then she repeats, "You only live once. And then, one day, just like that—it's gone."

"Hmm. I'm gonna ponder that."

"And you'll call me tomorrow?"

"To be honest, Sofia, I might not remember this. I drank a lot. And the drugs. . . ."

She reaches into my pocket and pulls out my phone and programs her number into my contact list. Placing it back in the palm of my hand, she kisses me again.

"I think you will."

I stand there on the front steps and watch as she enters the lobby without looking back. Will I forget this moment? What's the point of going out and meeting people if you have no recollection of it? How many times have I made a connection, promised to call somebody, only to never speak to them again? There are so many questions swirling around my head. I don't know how to feel. I wonder if Sofia and I would actually have any chemistry if we were sober, if we'd even be able to make it through a date, and why she chose me over an entire club of suitors. Many of them were better-looking and better-dressed. What did she see in me? What does anybody ever see in me? I hope I still remember her in the morning.

TWENTY-THREE

I'm sprinting down the sidewalk, trying to shake off the effects of the drugs and alcohol while searching for an ATM so I can buy some late-night food and pay for a cab home. As I'm running, I inadvertently trip over a pylon that's been left on a patch of weathered concrete. Angered, I pick up the pylon and hoist it above my head and attempt to throw it onto the roof of a nearby store. It almost reaches, but the base of the pylon catches the corner of the wall and it comes crashing down. I try another throw.

Same result. Then I hear a man shouting gibberish at me from across the street; he runs out in front of oncoming traffic and a taxi has to slam on the brakes to avoid plowing into him. He's rushing toward me. Why? I'm confused, in a daze, and all I see is a shadow, an apparition approaching me from the darkness. I hurl the pylon at him and yell "Eat pylon!" but my throw misses the target by several feet.

He's close now. I watch the shadow leap up onto the sidewalk and then his right hand shoots forth and hammers me on the left side of my face, slightly below the eye. I'm so numb from the alcohol that I barely feel any pain; I simply stagger backward and grab onto the shadow by his collar. To my surprise, this apparition is nothing more than a stocky, college-aged Korean kid with spiky black hair and a beige shirt. I cock my fist and press him up against the wall.

"Now why the fuck would you do that?" I shout. Maybe I accidentally flirted with his girlfriend tonight, or maybe his family owns this store, or maybe he just wanted to punch somebody—I don't know, but I'm guessing the latter. He gawks at me without answering. His mouth is wide open. His eyes appear vacant and stunned. He doesn't try to push me away or even raise his hands to defend himself. He doesn't react. I realize he might be even drunker than I am.

"I said, why did you do that?"

In the corner of my eye I see a girl running toward us. She grabs onto his arm and starts pulling with both hands, trying to drag him away from me, but I won't let him go. I want retribution. I want to imprint four knuckles into his goddamn forehead. But, for whatever reason, my arm begins to relax, and I refrain. I think about what happened earlier at the bar with Natalie and all the anger I felt and I look into her eyes and I can't bring myself to hit him. I let go of his collar and they both fall backwards to the ground. Then I slowly stumble away, watching as she scrambles to get him into a taxi.

When I reach up to feel my face, I find a swollen lump about the size of a quarter below my left eye and there's wet blood all over my fingertips. I didn't realize he had caused so much damage. Enraged, I run toward them, intent on evening the score, but they're already in a cab and driving away. I chase the car down the yellow line in the centre of the road until they're out of sight; my sprint gradually slows to a crawl and then I come to a standstill, admitting defeat. I pour some gin from my flask onto my hand and rub it into the wound and it stings, so I take another swig to ease the pain.

I need to wash this blood off my face. The lake can't be very far from here. I start heading toward the water, following the road south all the way across the bridge overlooking the old railway tracks and underneath the Gardiner Expressway. At the last intersection before the waterfront, a police van parks beside me as I'm waiting for the light to change. Inside, there are two officers; one of them pokes his head out through the passenger side window. He's balding with a comb-over and a big moustache.

"Hey you!" he hollers. "You're the one who's been kicking over all the mailboxes!"

"Uh . . . I'm pretty sure you've got the wrong guy."

"No! I know it was you." He pauses for a moment and examines my face. "What the hell happened to your eye?"

"Some asshole punched me! He's the guy you should be looking for. He's got spiky hair and a fat, stupid face."

"Oh, well then! We'll keep an *eye* out for him."

The two cops chuckle at each another.

"Can you give me a ride home?" I ask. "Or at least drive me to the bus stop?"

"No!"

"Well, I'm just gonna kick over more mailboxes then!"

"You better not!" he shouts as the van pulls away. I scan the intersection for any mailboxes, but, finding none, I cross the road and continue southward toward the water.

Past the sidewalk, I see a small metal sign nailed to a piece of wood resting a few inches off the ground marking a dirt path through the shrubbery. The sign reads: SPADINA QUAY WETLAND. I follow the path as it curves through the bush and leads me onto a stone walkway running alongside the waterfront. There are boats docked to the left of me and a small park to the right; I stumble as far as I can until I find six black benches at the end of a wide pier. With absolutely no energy left, I stretch out and collapse onto one.

The lake is calm and tranquil. To my right, a monolithic building once used by the Canada Malting Company looms heavily in the background, like a mummified corpse, stained yellow from time and rain and rust. Across the water, the lights of the island airport blink and flash, but all I can hear are the subtle waves pressing against the docks. I decide to remove my leather jacket and wear it like a blanket and suddenly I'm no longer cold. Before I fall unconscious, I feel my phone vibrating in my pocket: Doc is texting me to ask if I slept with the Armenian girl. No, I tell him—I'm actually lying on a pier bench and I might die here. By the time I press *Send*, my eyes are already closed.

TWENTY-FOUR

When I sleep, I dream Rachael is still alive. It's only when I wake that she disappears again. In my dreams, it was all a misunderstanding: she's alive and well and I was simply mistaken. It's the first day of July and we're watching fireworks go off by the water like we did when we were kids, and she's telling me about how they were better last year and the night sky is bright and clear.

In the real world there was no sign of Rachael anywhere. No phone calls, no emails, no trace of her left on the internet. Sometimes, when I was drunk in the middle of the night, I would type her name into search engines and find nothing. She trusted me with every password she ever had—occasionally, she would ask me to check her email for her when she was away from the computer—so once, late at night, I tried to login to her email account. The old password still worked. There were thousands of unread messages. She hadn't clicked on any of them. It wasn't a prank, a mistake or a delusion. She really was gone.

My father died nearly three years before she did. After his funeral, I locked myself in my room for several weeks. I received many consolatory messages from people saying things like "every-thing happens for a reason" and "he's in a better place now," but Rachael was the only person who actually came to visit. She took time off work and stayed with me, cramped inside my tiny apart-ment. I was living by the ocean at the time and one day we walked along a gravel path by the edge of the water and she sud-denly gave me a long hug. I asked her, "What was that for?" and she said, "Looked like you needed one." We were in our own lit-tle world. She told me things she said she would never tell any-one else. "Don't you trust anyone else?" I asked her. "No," she said. In our brief time together, I felt like I was at peace again. Like I was home.

Rachael talked me through it. She wasn't afraid to call me on my bullshit either, often criticizing me for trying to laugh every-thing off and keeping my feelings bottled inside. She said I was emotionally detached and she was right; I took stock of what she said and genuinely tried to improve, to get better. She encouraged me to be confident, to trust in myself, and she always stayed patient with me, despite my tendency to disappear for weeks at a time or to drive people away entirely. Somehow, we always came back to each other.

On the last day of her visit, I accompanied her to a hotel lobby where the airport shuttle bus was soon to arrive. We talked about when we'd see each other again and what we wanted to do in the future. It was a beautiful sunny day.

"If I could do anything, I'd run a coffee shop," she said. "I'd sell coffee by day, and you could turn it into a bar at night." I told her I liked the idea, but I wasn't ready to settle down in one place. I had to do something important first, something special, something that would make her proud, like become a musician or a journalist or travel the world working in international development. At the time, I thought I could do anything. That was the thing about Rachael: she made you feel like you could do anything.

"When I leave here, you're not gonna disappear for weeks again, are you?" she asked. "No," I said, "I'll be in touch." She told me I should have more faith in people, rely on them more, and not try to live through everything on my own. I responded with my usual stubborn posturing, assuring her I didn't need anybody. After losing my dad I didn't want to depend on anyone like that ever again. I thought relying on others made you weak. "I can take care of myself," I said. She tilted her head to the side with affection and perhaps a little pity and said my life sounded lonely.

The shuttle bus pulled into the driveway. I held her close as we said goodbye and then we kissed one last time. As she was walking out the door, she turned back to me and said, "You should come home."

"I will," I said. "But there are some things I want to do first."

"By yourself?"

"Yeah."

"I want to travel, too, but I wouldn't want to live anywhere else. I'd miss my family and friends too much." Then she paused for a moment before adding, "The timing never seems to work out for us."

She boarded the shuttle and I watched her take her seat and stare out the window as the bus drove away. I planned on inviting her to Toronto to see my new apartment once I settled in, but that never happened. And it never will.

I was lying on a pile of pillows and blankets in the centre of the room when I received a phone call from an old friend at three o'clock in the morning. He told me Rachael had died in her sleep. They didn't know why. She suffered from epilepsy and they thought it might be related to that. I hung up the phone and once again locked myself inside for weeks. I didn't go to the funeral. I couldn't eat, couldn't sleep, couldn't move. I tried listening to music, but nothing sounded right. It felt like my chest was hollow and I hated myself for not being there for her. For ten years she was the one constant in my life. Now, the memories of the time we spent together are only in my mind. Nowhere else. When I'm gone, those memories will disappear too, into thin air. Did they ever really happen? Did I dream them all? What if everything I remember about her was merely imagined?

TWENTY-FIVE

A month after Rachael died I grew tired of living like a recluse, so I loaded up the Widowmaker with a few essentials and drove south. It was sometime in August and the weather was warm. I had no plan or destination in mind—I just knew I wanted to get out of the city and be closer to the water. I didn't get very far. That first day, I came across a small town on the northern coast of Lake Erie called Turkey Point. A long beach ran alongside the main street from end to end, and separating the town from the sand was a metre-high wall made out of two layers of grey rock. I drove by a quaint motel with a green roof next to an old orange arcade and a food stand where they sold burgers, ice cream, poutine and two-dollar rounds of mini-putt. There was little else aside from the road, the sky and the water. Several boats had anchored a few yards away from the shoreline, proudly displaying flags of different provinces and countries. Some played the radio while their occupants jumped in and out of the water, while others were dead silent, reveling in the calm. I parked on the side of the road and found a spot at the edge of the beach where I leaned up against the rock wall wearing nothing more than a pair of blue trunks and sunglasses. Occasionally, I would go for a swim, but there was a lot of seaweed at the bottom of the lake and it slithered against my feet, so I mostly floated on my back and looked skyward.

On the second day, after having slept in my car overnight, I returned to the same spot and soaked in the sunshine. I passed the time by reading a collection of short stories by Ray Bradbury, including one called "The Lake," which I read and re-read several times. Suddenly, I heard someone call out from behind me, "Hey! You there! Can you help us out?" and I turned around to see a tanned, middle-aged man hollering at me from across the street. He had long, curly hair, an unkept goatee and a bare pot-belly. He and three other men, who were all so baked from the sun that their skin looked golden brown, were building a wooden frame for a new house. "We need a little help here, my man! It'll only take a second."

I closed my book and plodded through the sand, crossing the road to where they were working. The man gave me directions on where to stand and what to lift. I grabbed onto the bottom of the frame and he said, "Okay. On three. One—two—*three!*" and then the five of us mustered all of our combined strength to hoist that wooden monstrosity into the air. Eventually we managed to prop it upright, and I steadied it while they hammered it into place. "Phew, alright! Thanks a lot, my man." He extended his arm and I shook his hand.

"Let me know if you need anything else," I said. Then I returned to my spot on the beach and read my book and spent the next couple of hours lying alone in the sun.

At night the anxiety attacks returned. My heart was palpitating and there was a sharp, piercing pain inside my chest that I knew only alcohol could relieve. I went to the small pub inside the motel and expected the room to be full, but the place was nearly empty. Two elderly men were quietly watching a baseball game on TV and a group of forty-somethings had congregated at a table in the corner where the bartender was busy chatting with them. I pulled up a stool at the bar and hunched over the counter and proceeded to order several rum-and-cokes.

"Can I get another?" I asked the bartender. She unenthusiastically obliged me before heading back to the table to continue conversing with the locals. I was about to call it a night by ordering a bunch of shots and drinking them all in succession before passing out in the backseat of my car when I heard two people walk in. One of them was the long-haired, potbellied man from earlier, and the other was an even older fellow with a paper-thin frame, a green trucker's cap advertising a small town drywall company, and a denim jacket that smelled as if it had spent a lifetime smothered in cigar smoke. They approached the bar and the first man recognized me. "Hey! It's you again! How ya doing, buddy?" he asked, patting me on the back. "I owe you one. What're you having?" It was then I realized he reminded me of Jeff Bridges—albeit a loud, Canadian version.

"Oh, that's alright."

"No, I insist! Hey! Judy!" The bartender looked up from the table. "Can we get two Molsons? And put his next one on my tab."

"Only if you promise to actually *pay* that tab."

"I'll pay it when you . . . stop . . . lookin' so good!"

She laughed. "Flattery. Nicely done."

The man turned to me and extended his hand for the second time that day. "My name's Walton and this is my friend, Dick. Don't bother talking to him, though . . . he's a grumpy old cunt!"

I nearly spit the rum out of my mouth.

"Oh, piss off, Walt!" Dick replied. "I'm watching the game here."

"See?"

"I'm Ethan. Nice to meet you." I lifted my glass and nodded my head as if to say "cheers."

"Where're you from, Ethan?"

"Uh . . . I just moved to Toronto about a month ago, actually."

"Ooo, the Big Smoke! Did you come all the way out here by yourself?"

Normally, I might've been annoyed by someone like Walton, but, on that particular night, I was just happy to have somebody to talk to. I hadn't spoken to another soul in weeks.

"Yeah. I had to get outta there."

"Oh I would too, if I lived in Toronto. I'd run for the goddamn hills. A young guy like you shouldn't be sittin' here all by himself though. How old are you?"

"Twenty-three."

"Whoa! Twenty-three! At your age—Christ, we're talking thirty, forty years ago now—I was off backpacking through Europe. Me and my buddy brought a tent and we hitchhiked from place to place, sleeping in people's yards. We really knew how to keep it cheap. You ever been?"

"No. Not yet."

"Oh man, you gotta go! It's unreal. I've been back a few times since. You can hop from country to country like that" —he snapped his fingers— "and they're all different. Sweden was my favourite, bar none."

"Yeah? Why's that?"

"The women! They're all blonde, they can speak English, and they're super smart. I felt like I needed a master's degree just to keep up with 'em."

"So why the hell are you still in Canada?"

"Good fuckin' question! Well, I got married a few years back, so that means I have to stay away from the ladies now. Right, Judy?" he called out.

"Leave me out of it, Walt."

"Hear the way she talks to me?" He motioned to Dick. "She's almost as bad as this crusty son of a bitch!"

"Dammit, Walt!" Dick replied. "Shut up!"

I cracked up with laughter and Walton joined in.

"What about Amsterdam?" I asked. "I heard that's fun."

"Oh yeah, it definitely has character. You wouldn't know it to look at me, but I'm a fairly conservative guy." Dick snorted at that remark. "No, it's true. Ignore him. So I didn't even go to the red-light district until the last night I was there. Even then, I approached it with caution. First of all, I couldn't even find the goddamn place, but they actually have little signs on the road with little red lights to let you know where it is."

"Really?"

"Yeah! And so I'm walking through these alleyways and they have these goddamn supermodel girls behind these glass windows, and all these little eighteen-year-old American kids look like they're about to lose their shit!" He laughed. "Dick here would've had a goddamn heart attack. This old cocksucker hasn't had a hard-on since the moon landing!"

"Fuck you, Walton! I'm trying to enjoy the ballgame!"

An hour passed and I was feeling very buzzed. Dick was talking nonsense about how the moon landing was actually a government conspiracy to scare the Soviet Union into backing down in the arms race and how he could eventually achieve an erection if he really, really concentrated and got plenty of sleep the night before. Walton and I were snickering the whole time.

"What an asshole, huh?" Walton whispered to me.

"Christ, why do I put up with you?" Dick sighed.

Sensing an opportunity to gain some valuable life lessons from a couple of grizzled, seasoned veterans, I asked them, "So, if you guys were my age again, what would you do differently?"

"Don't get married!" cried Dick.

Walt shook his head. "Ah, don't listen to him—"

"No, trust me," Dick lamented, "you'll rue the day. I got tricked into it twice!"

"Yeah?"

"Twice. And the only person I hate more than my ex-wife . . . is my wife!"

The three of us laughed, and then clinked our glasses together. "And don't have children!" Dick continued. "For God's sake, they'll take away the best years of your life. Then you wake up one morning and you look like *this*." He pointed at his face and I was aghast. The thought of seeing that in the mirror every day made me shudder.

"Don't listen to him, Ethan," Walton assured me. "He's just bitter because his wife is an old bitch."

"Hey!"

"No, come on, Dick. She is. She is. But if you find the right girl, there's nothing wrong with gettin' hitched. Hell, I couldn't do it without Sandy. She's a little firecracker, that one. She's got a real Type A personality, y'know? It keeps me going. We've been married for, what, twelve years now? Wait, twelve? No. Thirteen."

"He doesn't even know!" shouted Dick.

Walton's comment about finding the right girl made me think of Rachael and I had to take another drink to alleviate the tightness in my chest. Fortunately, Dick and Walton kept my mind occupied; watching those two old assholes lob insults back and forth like a tennis ball was hypnotic.

Eventually Dick called for a brief intermission. As he strolled off to relieve himself, Walton told me, "In all seriousness, though, if I were your age, I'd get out there and see the world. See as much as you can now, 'cause when you get older, it becomes a lot tougher."

"I'd like to. I've wanted to travel . . . but I don't really have the money to do it."

"Well, you don't even have to go far! In Ontario, in Canada, there's so much that people never see. A few years back, my wife and I packed everything into a truck and went and saw the Rockies, the Prairies, the Maritimes. . . ."

"And Turkey Point?"

"And Turkey Point!" he repeated. "Anywhere you go, there's always something new, some place you hadn't seen before. And if you catch it on the right day, man, I tell ya, nature is medicinal. It can heal you."

I finished my glass and motioned to Judy for a refill.

"Whoa, you're really pounding those back, huh?" he said.

"Yeah. Long week."

"What do you do anyway?"

"Well, I just finished my first degree, but it's a bachelor of arts, so I can't really get a job with it. Nobody's lining up to hire me, put it that way. But I'm gonna study journalism in the fall."

He chuckled to himself. "Man, I've worked so many god-damn jobs over the years. Some of them good, some of them bad. The one thing I've learned is, just do what you love. Don't do it for the money. What's the point of having money if you're miserable forty hours a week? Life's too short. You don't need that much to get by, really, so keep it simple. Do what you liked to do when you were a kid."

I turned my head, looked him straight in the eye, and said, "No!"

Then we both laughed and took another swig.

"Or don't! I don't give a shit," he replied.

"When I was a kid, I liked playing Nintendo and hucking snowballs at cars."

"That was it, huh?"

"Basically. But building houses? That's what you like?"

"Oh yeah! I've always loved building shit. It's not like a desk job. At the end of the day, you can actually *see* what you've put together, all the fruits of your labour. It's rewarding."

Dick finally returned and sat down on his stool and Walton immediately glared at him. "Took you long enough! Does your pecker still work, you stupid codger?" With his eyes still fixated on the television, Dick held up his right hand and gave Walton the finger. The two of us were cackling again and I celebrated by ordering a couple of shots of whiskey for myself.

"Whoa! This kid's got the gene!" said Walton.

"What gene?" I asked.

"The booze gene. I've got it. Dick's definitely got it. You gotta be careful! That stuff'll kill you. Especially the hard stuff."

"Well, we all gotta go sometime." After taking another shot, I flagged down Judy and bought two more. "Duly noted though. These'll be my last two for the night."

"You've just gotta slow down, my man! You're chugging it down like it's water. Relax! Have a beer instead."

"I'll be fine," I slurred. "It's not like I have to go to job tomorrow." I took the first shot and pushed the glass forward and then held onto the second one by the rim and raised it into the air. "A toast! Here's to you and your lovely wives." Dick and Walton drank to that. I slammed the shot glass down onto the bar counter and reached for my wallet and paid Judy for all the liquor I had consumed. It was a steep bill.

As I prepared to leave, I said to Dick and Walton, "Thanks for the advice. It was nice meeting you guys."

"You too, my man." Walton replied, shaking my hand for a third time. "You gonna be alright?"

"Oh yeah. At ease, gentlemen," I said as I shuffled toward the exit. Suddenly, I felt a sharp pain in the pit of my stomach and a sweet taste at the back of my tongue—my body's signal that I was about to vomit. My walk accelerated into a sprint as I rushed through the door and ran toward a patch of grass at the side of the building where I heaved my innards onto the ground. The rum and whiskey burned my esophagus and stung my sinuses. Wiping my mouth, I stumbled across the road to the Widowmaker and struggled to find the keys in my pocket. Then I unlocked the door, collapsed into the backseat and awkwardly pulled a blanket over my torso before passing out, unconscious.

About an hour later I heard someone tapping on the car window, waking me from an uncomfortable sleep. I rolled over and saw Walton's face pressed against the glass, peering inside like that dinosaur from *Jurassic Park*. Dick was a step behind him. I dragged my upper body to the driver side door and opened it.

"Can I help you?" I said, still feeling groggy.

"Kid, are you sleeping in your fuckin' car?" Walton asked. Obviously, he already knew the answer.

"It's a lot roomier once you get inside. Like the Hilton and shit. Don't worry about me."

"Nah, my man, this won't do. You can't be sleeping out here like this. Come on, I got a pull-out couch back at the castle."

"Look, Walton, I appreciate the concern, but I sleep like this all the time. Besides, I can barely feel anything—"

"It's just around the corner. About a five-minute walk. Take one look, and if you don't like it, you can come back here and sleep like a goddamn hobo."

"No, I'll be fine. Thanks, though." I reached over and began to close the door.

"My old lady makes a really good breakfast. Belgian waffles, maple syrup, three-cheese omelettes, the works."

I stopped for a moment and realized I was hungry. I probably hadn't eaten a full meal in several days. "You had me at Belgian. Now help me up, would ya?"

Walton grabbed me by the arm and hoisted me to my feet as I closed the door behind me. We said goodnight to Dick, and then I stumbled behind Walton as he led me to his cottage, which he later explained actually belonged to his sister-in-law. The exterior was small and green with a driveway barely big enough for a single car. There were two steps leading up to the front door and the inside smelled of old wood and sawdust and the walls were decorated in maps and advertisements from the first half of the twentieth century. We had to be quiet because his wife was fast asleep; Walton showed me how to pull out the brown couch in the living room and then he fetched me a pillow and blanket before turning off the light and leaving through the hallway.

"Sleep it off, kid, and we'll see ya in the morning."

TWENTY-SIX

I awoke several hours later to an unfamiliar room and initially I had no recollection as to why I was there. It took me a moment to orient myself; I vaguely remembered the conversations with Walton and Dick, the shots of whiskey, the vomiting, the sleeping in the car and the subsequent walk to the cabin. Having become accustomed to the backseat of a car, the pull-out couch was a vast improvement, but I felt extremely dehydrated and desperately needed something to drink. I couldn't find my jeans on the floor, so I decided to carry on without them—the kitchen was only a few steps away anyway. After checking two of the cabinets, I eventually found a stack of green plastic cups and poured myself a glass of tap water. Then another one. And another.

As I was exhaling in relief, standing in the middle of the kitchen holding a cup of water and wearing nothing but my underwear, Sandy walked into the room. She gasped, clutched her chest and nearly jumped out of her morning gown. "Jesus Christ!" she cried.

I finished my sip before answering. "Walton told me I could stay here for the night," I said, pointing in the hypothetical direction of the master bedroom. "I'm Ethan." I held out my hand while she continued to glare at me for a few seconds before storming into the hallway and shouting "Walton!"

Perhaps I should have put on my pants. I heard them whispering in the other room as I searched for my missing jeans. I eventually found them underneath the pull-out couch and put them on one leg at a time. Sandy returned from the hallway as I was fastening my belt.

"Sorry about that," she said. "We're not used to having company." I stood there and examined her face for the first time and, like Walton, she looked as if she would have fit right in with the hippie generation. Time had worn her down a little, etched lines into her face and forced her to wear glasses, but she still had that glint in her eyes, that spark of energy. She must have been quite a catch in her day. "Let's try this again. I'm Sandy. Are you hungry?"

"Starving."

"Well, if you can hold out for half an hour, I'll whip up some food."

Sandy was true to her word. By the time I had smoked a cigarette outside on the deck, breakfast was served. The kitchen table was absolutely smothered in food: there were scrambled eggs, golden hash browns, smoked sausages, buttered toast, a bowl of sliced mango and cantaloupe, and whipped cream and chocolate syrup for the waffles. I thought I'd died and gone to heaven. I hadn't eaten a breakfast like that in years—typically I would just toast a bagel or pour a bowl of cereal because my stomach would be too upset to digest any real food, but not that day. Seizing the opportunity, I wolfed it down.

"Sorry for the surprise, sweetheart," said Walton. "I didn't wanna wake you up last night only to tell you that Ethan here would be using our couch."

"Oh, it's alright," she sighed. "I just thought he was an axe-murderer."

"The fact that he was half-naked didn't tip you off, huh?" Walton joked.

I looked up and smiled while still chewing fervently.

She smiled too. "Nope! I was thinking he might be a perv or something." Then she turned to Walton and said, "Next time, a little heads-up would be appreciated."

"I figured I'd wake up before you."

When we finished eating, I volunteered to do the dishes but Sandy was already scrubbing them in the sink. Walton told us he had to drive into Simcoe to pick up some supplies from the hardware store, and he offered to drop me off at my car.

"No, that's okay," I said. "I can walk."

"Nonsense! I'm going that way anyway. Come on."

I cleaned up the living room and thanked Sandy for her hospitality, and she told me I could come back for waffles anytime. Walton drove me down the road to my car and then he turned off the ignition and we sat there quietly in his truck.

"So, where're you off to next?" he asked.

"I don't know. Probably head back to Toronto."

"What about your family? Where do your parents live?"

"They divorced when I was eight. My old man died a few years back, and my mom lives out of the country. We don't see each other much."

"Jeez, I'm sorry, kid. But you can't be sleeping out here in your car forever." He paused. "Just do me a favour, would ya? Go easy on the booze. I used to be a lot like you—until I learned how to ease up. And it got me into a lot of trouble."

"What kind of trouble?"

"Man, you name it. With the law, with my family, with my first wife . . . I couldn't even hold down a job. I was just young and angry and lashing out at everything, like a bull seeing red. Then, one day, I woke up with a hangover so bad I couldn't take it anymore. Couldn't do it to myself again. If that day ever comes for you, remember it. Etch it into your brain. Find a way to remind yourself every goddamn day what it felt like to be at that point. To not have a single friend left in the world. Rock bottom. Trust me, you'll never want to feel that way again."

I stayed silent, so he continued: "Alcohol's a double-edged sword, my man. Some of the best times I ever had were when I was piss-loaded. But a lot of bad things happened too. It's funny, of all the places, I met Sandy at a bar. She was sitting there with a friend of hers and I was knocking back the hard stuff with a buddy of mine and we eventually got to talking. If I hadn't been drinking at the bar that night, I probably never would've met her."

I think I understood what he was trying to say. Our successes, our mistakes, even our failures, when they're all added together over the course of a lifetime, they ultimately lead us to where we're supposed to be.

"Thanks for everything, Walt."

"And hey, don't worry if you don't have everything figured out yet. At your age, you're not supposed to. Here, I'll give you my card. You gimme a call if you ever need any construction work done or anything else."

I stepped out of the truck and got back into my car and watched as Walton waved and honked the horn twice before driving off in the opposite direction. I opened the glove compartment and placed his card inside and then reached across the passenger seat to retrieve an old yellow map of Ontario. I unfolded the map and planned my route back to Toronto and started driving. A few months later I met Doc and sold my car to him and I haven't left the city since.

—Part III—

White Mice & Roses

Hollywood always gets it wrong. Alcoholism isn't about seeing pink elephants or having hallucinations about bats chasing mice. The pathetic fallacy that it's always dark and raining when you're hungover is completely untrue. In reality, the hardest mornings are when the sun is shining and you wish you could feel it, be a part of it, but you can't because you're bedridden and buried beneath a mound of blankets. It's like being in limbo, comatose, in a cocoon. Survival requires you to work around the addiction, to try to tame it, to work it into your schedule and live with it. Once you've gotten used to the lifestyle, it would be impossible to revert overnight. But that's what happens in the movies. They wrap it up nicely in the third act. The alcoholic simply decides not to drink anymore. Problem solved. But they're missing the point entirely. In my experience, alcoholism is a *symptom*—a symptom of a much deeper disease.

For me, it's a social crutch, an excuse, a painkiller and an escape. Sometimes it works in your favour, but you can easily take things too far and do and say things you ultimately regret. You can act carelessly and admit you don't remember anything and people will forgive you once, maybe twice, but you can only apologize so many times before your words become empty and hollow. Eventually that becomes the only person they know, and they have no choice but to cut you loose, leaving you feeling all the more dejected, isolated and lonely. For me, alcohol provides a temporary relief from the boredom, the emptiness, the constant pain in my chest and the sleepless nights—all of which are caused by the fundamental feeling that something is *wrong* with the world. Something is seriously fucked up. And I don't fit into it.

I'm sleeping on a bench at the end of a pier when I'm suddenly awoken by the sound of Doc's voice. He's kneeling beside me, trying to shake me back into consciousness. "Hey! Reid! Come on, man, wake up!" He lifts my shoulders off the bench, forcing me into a seated position, and my eyes gradually begin to open. Then he passes me a bottle of water and I try to drink from it, but the water seeps down the back of my throat and I cough.

This isn't the first time he's come to help me. Last winter, I was stumbling home from a bar one night when I got lost in the midst of a violent snowstorm. I trudged through the ice and blowing snow and tried to make it back to my apartment, but to no avail. Eventually, I became enervated by the cold and my legs failed me and I collapsed into a snowbank. Before I fell unconscious, I called Doc and told him where I was and said that I might freeze to death. He immediately hailed a cab and within minutes found me lying deep in the snow. The cab driver refused to take me because he thought I might vomit or die in the backseat of his car, so Doc propped me up by the shoulder and carried me all the way home. I've cheated death like that probably a dozen times. Yet, somehow, I was still alive while so many more deserving people lay cold in the ground or with their ashes stored in urns above the fireplace. It's an unjust world.

"Give me a minute," I groan. "I'm not ready to go yet."

"Sure," he says, slumping down on the bench beside me.

This is the hangover Walton warned me about. Although I can barely recall anything, there is an inherent feeling of guilt and embarrassment constricting my entire body. Then I remember the awful text messages I sent to Natalie. The uncertainty makes my heart clench and tighten. My bones ache and my eye is swollen and my nose is clogged and runny. The discomfort is inescapable, excruciating. I never want to feel this way this again. He was right.

Doc tells me it's almost six o'clock in the morning and the sun should be rising soon, somewhere over the lake. Even now, I can see the first signs of daylight as the sky gradually changes from pitch black to powder blue.

"What the hell happened to your eye?" he asks.

I shake my head without answering.

"Did you punch him back?"

"No."

Pause.

"Did you sweep the leg?"

"No, I didn't *sweep the leg*!"

A few moments pass.

"Man, I feel old," I say.

"I know, man. Me too."

"You realize it's been, like, seven years since we left high school? Our ten-year reunion is coming up soon."

"That's crazy. . . . I don't know where the time went."

"There's no way I'd ever go to the reunion. I haven't done anything I wanted to do since then. . . . I just drank and took some classes. I wouldn't know what to tell people."

"Me neither. But nobody else from my school has done anything either. I mean a few of them have jobs, but nothing special."

"But how many of them are married now? Or have kids? I can't imagine having kids at this age."

"I'd be terrible at it."

"Yeah. Maybe when I'm, like, thirty-five. But now? Shit, I still feel eighteen."

"Me too."

Another long pause.

"Remember the days when we didn't have to be loaded drunk to have a good time?" I say. "When you could just play basketball or video games on a Friday night and still have fun?"

"Yeah, man! Me and my friends used to play ball hockey every day after school. I'd totally be up for it if other people were. Why don't we do that anymore?"

"Nobody has any equipment."

"Still, that can't be hard to come by."

"Yeah . . . I miss those days."

I brandish the hip flask from my pocket.

"There's still a bit left," I say. "Want some?"

I pass the flask to Doc and he takes a swig. Then he exhales and hands it back to me and I do the same. A moment later we spot a police boat patrolling the harbour in the distance.

"Think they'll mind?" I ask.

"Nah, fuck 'em."

Doc takes the flask from my hand and holds it up high in the air, waving it at the boat. Then he drinks from it again. Time passes slowly as we sit there gazing into the water. The waves gently rock back and forth like a cradle and I can hear seagulls cawing on the other side of the channel.

"Man, if my ten-year-old self could see me right now, he'd be so pissed off," I say.

Doc laughs. "Same."

"I thought I would've done so much more by now. Orson Welles was working on *Citizen Kane* when he was our age. Neil Young wrote 'Old Man.' What have I done?"

"Man, we've still got time. We should just *go* somewhere. Go to fucking Asia and teach English or something. . . ."

"I knew a guy at my old job who did that. I think he went to Japan? He said it was awesome."

"See? Why don't we do that?"

"I don't know. He also said it was kinda like . . . putting your life on hold. You make a bit of money, you get to live in a different country, but eventually you've gotta come home. And when you do, all the same shit is still here waiting for you, only now you're a year older."

Doc considers for a moment. "Still, it'd be better than staying here and doing nothing, wasting our lives. . . ."

"Maybe. . . . I know I can't keep doing this every night, going out and drinking like this. What's the point? I just end up spending a bunch of money and feeling like shit the next day anyway. And even if I meet a girl, I usually never see them again, so what's the point of that? The hangovers keep getting worse and worse, too—some days I can't even get out of bed until, like, four in the afternoon. Honestly, it's not even fun for me anymore. I don't have a job, I don't know *what* the hell I'm doing in school, I'm running out of money. . . ."

Doc nods his head and looks down at his feet for a while before saying, "Well, I'm gonna get that teaching certificate. Then I'm gonna look into one of those programs. Some of them even pay for your flight and accommodations."

"Yeah, I remember you talking about it. Don't you have to sign a one-year contract though?"

"I think so."

"I don't know if I could do a whole year. . . ."

"Ah, c'mon, man. A year will fly by. What's keeping you here?"

I try to think of an answer, but take too long to respond.

"You've been to Hong Kong before, right?" he asks.

"Yeah. My old man took me when I was twenty."

"We could go there? They must need teachers?"

"I don't know, man. . . ."

"Well, I'm doing it. I'm definitely going. If not Asia, then somewhere else. And you should too."

In lieu of answering, I glance over at Doc and grin and then lift up the flask and finish the last remnants of alcohol. We both stare out at Lake Ontario and watch as the sun rises over the horizon and the city begins to wake once more.

TWENTY-EIGHT

Doc helps me to my feet and tells me he's driving to the family cottage in Kincardine to visit his oldest sister Karen, her husband Charlie and their three-year-old son Jacob. He invites me to come along—says a ride through the countryside and a decent meal might help with the hangover. I reluctantly accept. It's not like I have anything else to do today. And it'll be nice to get out of the city for a change. It's been almost a year since I last got out.

The Widowmaker is parked on the lot next to the pier and the headlights are still on. When I open the door, I remember the passenger side window is broken and I can't help but feel partially responsible. Doc turns the key in the ignition and we start driving; there are a few early morning joggers and the occasional taxi, but aside from that the city is calm. Doc must be groggy—he probably didn't get a wink of sleep—but he assures me he's okay to drive and I'm in no position to argue. We move north on Jarvis

Street up to Mount Pleasant Road and a few minutes later we're parked outside my apartment. "I'll wait here," he says. "Get everything you need. And take as long as you want, I don't care."

I enter the lobby and ride the elevator and unlock the door to my apartment. The air inside feels stale, as if the windows haven't been opened for days, and the daylight is barely visible between the gaps in the blinds. Normally, I'd be huddled in bed right now, completely immobilized, but today is different. I have a second wind. I open my closet door and snatch a change of clothes and a pair of sunglasses and stuff them into an old backpack. Then I go into the bathroom and grab my toothbrush, a comb, a stick of deodorant and a towel. As I'm walking out, I catch a glimpse of myself in the mirror for the first time since last night and I'm horrified to see the large pink circle surrounding my left eye. It looks like it's turning purple, and there's a deep, rounded cut underneath. He must have been wearing a ring, maybe two rings, because there's another long cut above my eyebrow. The wound is throbbing and I need a painkiller; almost instinctively, I reach into my jacket pocket and pull out the bottle of codeine. I hold it there in my hand, studying the label for a moment, and then I think about what Walton said to me a year ago and I realize I don't want to have anything to do with this stuff anymore. I'm tired of it. All of it. I toss the codeine into the trash and then open the medicine cabinet and drop more bottles, one by one, into the same bin. By the end of it, the shelves are nearly empty, save for a few vitamin supplements and some ibuprofen. I take two ibuprofen—the recommended dosage—and swallow.

Before leaving, I decide to pick up some of the dirty clothes on the floor and throw them into the laundry basket. Then I stack the pizza boxes, organize the liquor bottles, make the bed and scrub a few of the dishes in the sink. What a difference it makes. I also make sure to grab an ice pack from the freezer and wrap it up in a paper towel. Everything is organized and ready to go, but I can't find my camera. I check my desk before rummaging through the hallway closet where I eventually locate it on one of the shelves. On the shelf below I notice an old photo album with three individual books I haven't looked at in a very long time. I open the first book to the first page and there are random shots of me taken by my father when I was about eight years old. I'm at a public playground and I'm going down slides, hanging upside-down on monkey bars and throwing a little yellow football around. My hair is blonde and bright and my adult teeth are coming in crooked. I seem happy. I was a completely different person back then. Looking at that kid makes me smile.

Wedged between two of the books is an old postcard dated from when I was fourteen. It's from Rachael. There's a picture of a wildlife zoo and a polar bear on the front. I can't believe I've held onto it for all these years. The postcard reads: *Ethan! Where are you? Why are you not at home? I mean, it's nice to visit your family and all, but wouldn't you rather talk to me? I'm joking, of course. Hope you're having a great time. I have lots of stories to tell you when you get back. Rachael.*

For a moment I consider throwing the postcard and all of the photos into the trash and starting over. There are some things in life I don't want to remember. While the thought is temporarily comforting, I can't bring myself to let them go. I leave the pictures where they are, safely stored on the closet shelf, and put the postcard in my backpack and leave through the apartment door. Downstairs, Doc is waiting for me in the driver's seat sleeping with his face pressed against the window. I knock on the glass to wake him up before getting into the car and tossing my bag into the backseat. I realize a night in the countryside probably won't be enough—I want to stay for a couple days, maybe weeks, and clear my mind.

TWENTY-NINE

Following a brief stop at a gas station where we buy sports drinks, potato chips, meat sticks and a few other necessities, we're soon on the road heading west. Doc brought his iPod for the trip and he fumbles with it while driving, eventually settling on "Blueprint" by Fugazi. My chair is reclined and my right foot is resting on the open window as I slide the ice pack underneath my sunglasses to relieve the swelling. Our clothes are dirty and my eye still hurts, but with the sun now fully awake and rising in the eastern sky, its light gently warming my face, I'm starting to feel a little better. The cool morning air blows against us and renews our senses and the memory of last night begins to stray from the forefront of my mind. Most of the traffic is moving eastbound—probably returning to the city after a weekend in cottage country—but we're swimming against the current. Doc keeps the car moving a little over a hundred kilometres per hour, coasting behind a big SUV in the right lane. He's too tired to drive aggressively or even carry on a conversation. So am I.

I stare out at the roads and the concrete as we drive past strip malls and industrial parks on our way through the suburbs. Eventually the highway narrows to six lanes and the buildings and noise barriers are gradually replaced by rolling hills and trees and farmland. We're finally out. I close my eyes and manage to catch up on some sleep as we coast alongside Milton and Campbellville. By the time my eyes open again, we're already in Guelph turning left on Woodlawn Road. I see a few stores and fast-food restaurants and car dealerships and a big movie theatre before Doc takes a right onto Highway 86 toward Elmira. He asks me if I need to stop for a bathroom break and I tell him "No" and he says "Good."

There's barely any traffic for miles in either direction. We pass a few solitary houses in the countryside and I think about how different it must be to live in the middle of nowhere, miles away from your nearest neighbour. I can see the appeal. Later, we speed past a traditional horse-and-carriage trotting on the shoulder and Doc tells me, "We're now entering Mennonite country." I ask him about the Mennonites and he explains how they shun automobiles and electricity and make their own clothing. "They fixed my uncle's roof for free one time," he says. "He woke up and they were already working on it. Nice people." As I'm quietly reflecting on their pastoral lifestyle, I'm suddenly overwhelmed by the smell of horseshit wafting into the car and, sadly, we can't roll up the window.

A blue sign tells us we're approaching a small town called Dorking and I throw a piece of gum at it as we pass. Rural Ontario is full of these tiny farming communities; most of them only have one intersection with an old brick church and maybe a general store. The road is straight as an arrow and Doc barely has to touch the steering wheel. I notice he hasn't spoken for several minutes and I imagine the nostalgia is beginning to set in for him; his family has been coming up to Kincardine every summer since he was born, so he's probably driven this road more times than he can remember. As we're approaching Listowel, my eyelids begin to feel heavy again and I slowly drift off to sleep.

Sometime later I feel the car come to a stop and the engine turn off. I hear Doc open the door. When I open my eyes I'm surprised to see an elementary school with an outdoor basketball court. The court itself is cracked and fractured, the painted lines having long since faded, and neither hoop has any mesh on the rim. Doc stands outside the car and says to me, "Hey! Wake up! Come out here for a sec." Then he moves around to the back of the car and pops open the trunk and retrieves a basketball. I watch as he casually shoots the ball at the nearest hoop and it hits the right side of the rim and bounces away.

"Come on!" he calls out to me.

Reluctantly I get out of the car. My knees are stiff from having been cramped inside for so long. I stroll over to the court and he passes me the ball and I catch it in my chest.

"This is stupid, Jeff."

"No it isn't. C'mon! Take a shot."

"I'm too hungover for this—"

"Shoot the fuckin' ball, Reid!"

Doc glares at me, waiting impatiently, so I grudgingly hold the ball in my right palm and steady it with my fingertips as I squint my eyes and line up the shot. My knees bend and release like a coiled spring as I hop an inch off the ground and toss the ball into the air on a perfect arc. It misses the backboard entirely and rolls off onto the grass. Doc retrieves the ball and passes it back to me.

"Okay, let's try that again," he says.

I look at him skeptically before repeating the process. This time the ball hits the lower part of the rim and quickly bounces right back into my hands. I pass it over to him.

"Your turn."

Doc misses wide again and catches his own rebound. Then, in frustration, he launches the ball overhand and it hits the top of the backboard and flies several metres away from the court.

"Man, we suck!" he notes.

"Nah. We're just out of practice."

He pauses. "This'll be really embarrassing if I ever have a kid."

I laugh. "You should never have a kid."

"No, I shouldn't," he admits.

As time goes on, we gradually improve to the point where we can score on roughly a third of our shots. I remember how to do a right-handed lay-up and begin to put them in consistently; I'm taller and stronger than I was in elementary school, though, so my brain has to adjust to the size difference, using less energy than it did years ago.

Ten to twenty minutes pass, and then we pick up the ball and start walking back to the car. Suddenly, Doc taps me on the upper arm and points to the school. Apparently somebody left the back door wide open. I follow behind him as he peers through the doorway to reveal an empty gymnasium with hardwood floors, clean basketball nets and a big stage. We cautiously wander inside and our footsteps echo. There's no one else around.

"What're we doing?" I ask him.

"Shh!" he whispers. "Maybe it's unlocked. . . ."

Doc tiptoes toward the utility room door and fiddles with the metal handle. When the knob turns, he smiles at me in disbelief and opens it slowly. The room is filled to capacity with colourful sporting equipment: soccer balls, baseball bats, hula hoops, jumping ropes, plastic scoops, red dodge balls, little wooden scooters—everything we used to play with as kids. Doc rubs his hands together in excitement and then finds a plastic hockey stick with an orange blade on the wall and tosses it to me.

"I'll go in net," he says.

He puts on a white goalie mask and a baseball glove and then we set up a hockey net below the stage. I fold a curve into the blade of the stick and use it to move a tennis ball around on the floor. When Doc is ready, I try to shoot it past him. Every time he makes a save, he calls out in triumph; anytime I score, he screams profanity. Like with basketball, our skills are rusty, but over the course of ten minutes our ability steadily returns and I remember how to shoot and stickhandle and fire a wrist shot.

Doc challenges me to a best-of-five shootout: five penalty shots where the stake of the game is hypothetical world domination. I miss wide on the first chance, but score through his legs on the next two. He curses at me and dares me to try it again; I ignore him and shoot it toward the top corner on his glove side instead. He does the splits and catches the ball, spinning his arm around like a windmill.

"Ha! Patrick Roy, motherfucker!" he shouts at me.

The pressure is on for the fifth and final shot. We're tied at two points each. The world is at stake. I deke the tennis ball to my right, to my backhand, and then to my right again. He crouches and prepares to make the save. I fake the shot, he flinches, and so I roll the ball softly between his feet and into the mesh at the back of the net.

"Goddammit!" he yells. Then he throws his stick to the floor in disgust and says, regrettably, "The world is yours."

"Sweet."

"Go again?"

"Yeah, sure."

Suddenly we hear footsteps reverberating through an adjacent hallway. A tall man wearing a white baseball cap, a white shirt, red shorts and a pair of clean running shoes marches into the gymnasium. Like a stereotypical gym teacher, he has a whistle hanging from his neck and a wooden clipboard in his hand. I expect animosity, but his face is smiling and amicable.

"Hey guys!" he announces. "You here for the summer camp?"

Doc shuffles nervously. I know he's about to spill the beans and tell the coach that we trespassed in here just to use and perhaps steal his sporting equipment, but my first instinct is to lie. Fortunately, I beat him to it.

"Yes. Yes, we are," I say confidently.

"You're a bit early. I don't think the kids are due for another two hours," he explains. "You brought a change of clothes, right? You're not really dressed the part." I glance down and realize I'm still wearing grey jeans and brown shoes.

"Yeah, we brought shorts," I say.

"So, which one of us hired you guys?" he asks.

"Uh . . ," I mumble in an attempt to stall for time. I look over at Doc and he stares back at me with widened eyes. I try to think of a common male name. "Mike?"

"Mike? Are you sure?"

"Something like that. Started with an M."

"Hmm. I don't know a Mike. What'd he look like?"

"Uh . . . brown hair? He had sort of a . . . round face . . . with very, uh, robust features."

"Really? That doesn't sound like anybody I know."

"Well, to be honest, his face wasn't *that* robust."

"Hmm. What did you say your names were again?"

Doc and I both turn to each other with the same startled expression. His body language is leaning toward the back door and I silently concur. "Abort!" I yell, and we drop our sticks and start sprinting toward the exit, running as fast as we can through the doorway and into the parking lot. Doc scrambles to unlock the car.

"Come on, man!" I shout.

"I'm trying!" he replies, fiddling with the keys while still wearing the baseball glove on his hand. He discards the glove and opens the door and we quickly start the car and fishtail out of the parking lot. The coach comes outside just in time to see us speeding off in a trail of dust and smoke. He looks baffled and confused.

"Woo!" I holler as we drive away. "That was awesome."

"Man, that was hilarious! I thought he was gonna kill us."

"Same. Sorry I'm not a better liar."

"Uh . . . Mike?" he imitates mockingly. "Nice try though."

Once the adrenaline abates, I say, "Thanks for taking me there, by the way."

"No problem. I haven't played ball hockey in forever. We've gotta do that more often."

"What, break into schools?"

"Yeah."

"Agreed."

THIRTY

It's midday and we're relaxing on patio chairs overlooking a beach on Lake Huron. Neither Karen nor Charlie ask me about my swollen eye upon meeting me. Maybe they think it's a birthmark. Charlie barbecues hamburgers and hotdogs on the deck and offers me a beer, but I decline, opting for water instead. Doc happily takes the beer. We also snack on a bag of cheese curds we bought from a farm and they're so fresh they squeak against my teeth. Charlie asks us about our drive to the cottage and we make small talk about how great the weather is and how the Blue Jays have been playing this season; Karen tells us their son Jacob is napping, but he'll soon wake up and come say hello.

Charlie is older than I thought he would be. Karen looks mature, even though she's only thirty years old, but he must be on the other side of forty. His hair is long and beginning to grey and his face appears tired and worn. When he speaks, his voice is calm and assured, but there's a listlessness in his eyes, like a light that's been extinguished. Still, he's friendly and talkative and seems fairly well-read. He helps us unload the car and bring our bags into the guest rooms and the inside of the cottage is larger than I imagined. There are hardwood floors and big windows and the smell of old wood and nature permeate the place. In the living room, several pieces of dusty furniture are situated around a neglected television and a few bookshelves, one of which is stacked with board games. The three of us sit at a table outside and play a game of cribbage with an antique pegboard and I manage to squeak out a victory in the first round, but Charlie wins the second round handedly. Frustrated, Doc knocks over all the pegs and refuses to partake in a rubber match. Then, in an act of defiance, he breaks the board over his knee and tosses it into the lake.

Later, while Doc is napping in his room, Charlie and I have a smoke outside on the deck while staring at the scattered waves. He's got a bottle of beer in one hand and a perfectly rolled joint in the other and he asks me if I want to partake with him.

"Thanks, but I'm alright," I say. "I'm still recovering from last night."

He lights the joint with a match and inhales before asking, "So, how'd you get that shiner?"

"Got punched in the face. But you should see the other guy!"

"Yeah?"

"He looks *great*."

Charlie laughs. "You didn't get him back, huh?"

"No. I had him by the collar, but for some reason I held back."

"Hmm. Probably for the best. It doesn't look too bad."

"Yeah, it should heal pretty quick, maybe in a week or two."

A few moments pass and then Charlie, perhaps in an enlightened state of mind due to the cannabis, says, "If I asked you about a midlife crisis—what do you think that is?"

Initially, I'm staggered by the question, but I can see in his eyes that he's earnest for an honest conversation. People rarely try to initiate a real dialogue with me, so I'm pleased whenever it happens. "I guess it's about regretting the decisions you've made."

"Karen . . . she complains I'm not the same guy she married. The guy she met six years ago."

I can't think of anything to say, so I just nod and listen.

"Let me prepare you for the midlife crisis," he says calmly, exhaling smoke. "When you're twenty, you really don't know what you're doing. You go out, you try to have fun, you meet people, but it's all pretty aimless until you reach thirty. Then it hits you, and you start to figure it all out—who you are, what you want, where you should be. But you only *really* know for sure around the time you turn forty. The sad reality is, by that time, you're too old to act, to take advantage of what you've learned. You're kinda . . . at the mercy of the life you've already created for yourself. And *that's* where the frustration comes from. You finally know what you want, but you're no longer in a position to get it. So, do I regret the decisions I made in my twenties? No, not really. Because the truth is . . . I never really made any."

At that moment, Karen walks through the sliding doors holding three-year-old Jacob by the hand. "Somebody wants to say hello," she says as Jacob runs at us and leaps onto his father's lap. Charlie quickly snuffs out the joint into a nearby ashtray and cradles his son in his arms.

"Did you meet Ethan yet?"

I smile and wave at Jacob. He gawks at me.

"What happened to your eye?" he asks inquisitively.

"I got hit with a baseball."

He points at my eyebrow.

"You're cut!"

"It was a *sharp* baseball."

He grins and hops onto the grass and starts running around.

"Hey, Jacob, show Ethan your exercise program," says Charlie.

Jacob looks at me with a stern expression on his face while puffing out his cheeks and extending his arms as far as they'll go. Then he starts spinning around in a circle like a top. After three seconds he gets dizzy and goes completely limp and collapses face-up on the ground. He lies there motionless a moment and then begins to giggle and we all laugh.

"Very nice," says Charlie as he casually applauds. "He's a great kid."

Jacob stands up and runs over to me, jumping onto my stomach and nearly knocking the wind out of me. Then he puts his arms around my neck and gives me a big hug. I don't know how to act around children; they typically make me uncomfortable because you can't swear or smoke around them and they're always noisy and shitting everywhere, but this kid seems alright. He has a nice personality and great parents and a decent chance of turning into a normal, well-adjusted human being. With his arms still gripping my neck, I give him a pat on the back and say, "Thanks, buddy. You're alright."

He smiles and hops off my chair and runs inside.

"He's a real great kid," Charlie repeats. "Tons of energy. Happy and smiling all the time. Never whines. The people at the daycare just love him."

"Yeah. He's gonna do fine."

THIRTY-ONE

I'm crouching at the edge of the guest room bed, rummaging through my backpack in search of my phone. When I find it, I'm dismayed to see the battery is nearly empty and I forgot to bring the charger. I decide to scroll through the contact list and scribble a few numbers into a notebook in case I need them later. Then I come across a new entry from last night: Sofia. I stare at it a moment and wonder who the hell Sofia is before the clouded image of her face reappears in my mind. While the memory is obscured, I can barely recall the colour of her hair and the sound of her voice and standing in front of her building as we parted ways in the early hours of the morning.

I turn off my phone and walk into Doc's room and ask him if there's a landline I can use.

"Only if it's a local call," he answers. "I don't want my parents getting any long distance charges. They'll blame me and that's the *one* thing I stand against. Is it a local call?"

"No."

"Fuck!" he says. "Alright."

He shows me to an old rotary phone on a nightstand in the corner before leaving the room and closing the door behind him. I push my finger into the metal circle and turn the dial and let it roll all the way back into place and then repeat the process for ten more digits. The phone rings. Adrenaline kicks in and I'm scratching at the hairs on the back of my neck.

"Hello?"

"Hi, Sofia? This is Ethan. I know it's kind of a weird time to call, but—"

"I'm sorry, who?"

"Ethan. From last night?"

Her voice sounds tired and desiccated, as if she's still lying in bed half-asleep. "Oh, right. Ethan."

My initial enthusiasm begins to shrivel. "We met at that after-hours bar, I think? Then I walked you home."

The line is silent for a moment. "Oh, yeah. I drank so much. I'm sick now. It's hard to know what I was doing."

Well this is ironic. She barely remembers me. I guess it would be hypocritical of me to get upset. I never should have called. We'd never work in the real world anyway.

"It's cool," I mumble nonchalantly. "Happens to me all the time. You should, uh, drink some water and sleep it off. Hopefully you'll feel better soon."

"Okay. I'm sorry. Call me again some other time, okay?"

"Will do."

I slowly hang up the phone. When I walk outside to the back of the cottage I find Doc sitting on the beach by himself. He's squinting at the lake and casually sipping a bottle of beer while occasionally skipping stones across the water. Heavy clouds have temporarily blocked out the sun and it looks like it might rain. I light a cigarette and take a seat on the sand beside him.

"Hey."

"Yo. Who'd you have to call?"

"That girl from last night."

"Oh yeah? How'd it go?"

"She's still asleep."

"Shit, I don't blame her. We were out pretty late."

We fall silent a moment. Doc keeps skipping stones, and they bounce once or twice along the surface of the water before getting lost in the waves. I hunch forward so that my arms are resting on my knees and say, "I was thinking about what we talked about earlier. You know, about high school."

"What about it?"

"It was all bullshit, wasn't it? I wish I'd known. If only I could go back and tell myself, 'Look, here's how it is. As soon as you leave this place, you'll never see any of these people ever again. They'll forget about you and you'll forget about them, so focus on what you want to do *after* school instead of wasting time worrying about girls or grades or any of that shit.' They tried to make it seem so much more important than it really was, y'know? I mean, I remember when I used to watch TV shows about kids in high school—they were all played by actors in their twenties and they hung out in restaurants all day and there were never any scenes where they were *actually* in class 'cause that'd be boring. Nobody ever had braces or breakouts or looked awkward like they do in real life and then, on Sunday mornings, they'd play those teen movies from the eighties with the sappy soundtracks. And so, after years of watching all that, I remember when I actually got to high school, I expected it to be so much better than it really was. Instead, it was just fucking *boring*. I spent most of the time staring at the clock and waiting for the day to end, or sitting on the goddamn floor in the hallway between classes. Even on weekends we'd just drive around drinking beer and smoking cheap cigars in parking lots until one day, just like that, it was over. We graduated and we had the prom and it's supposed to be some big deal, the most important night of our lives, but Rachael and I had an awful time and it was over and done with before I knew it. We all said we'd keep in touch, but everybody kinda forgot about each other as soon as we left. I bet most of them wouldn't even remember me now. So now I'm thinking, 'Why the hell did I care so much in the first place?' Later, I go to college, and I think, 'Well, it's gonna be like *Animal House*,' y'know, with drunken toga parties and that song 'Louie Louie' and all that kinda shit, and I remember I showed up at the residence on the first night, and it's a Friday night, and so I expect everybody to be getting drunk and being social, but when ten o'clock rolls around they're all just sitting in their rooms talking to their friends back home on their computers. Shit, we weren't even *allowed* to drink legally until we were nineteen, so I usually had to pay an older kid to buy me booze so I could chug two-dollar tall-boys of this disgusting ten-percent beer in my shitty dorm room, which was barely big enough to fit a mattress. So then I go looking for something better, and I move onto different cities and go to different schools, but the story is always the same, and I always end up drinking at a bar by myself. I finally get my degree only to find out it's not worth the paper it's written on because nobody gives a shit about a bachelor of arts anymore—you need a masters degree or a PhD and even *then* they might not care—they give away bachelor degrees to anyone who's got the time and money and can answer a few multiple-choice questions. So then I try to go out and get a regular job, like normal people, but nobody will hire me because I don't have any experience 'cause I just spent the last six years of my life in school trying to figure out what the hell I wanted to do. I can't even get a monkey's job at the mall because, for some reason, the piece of shit manager doesn't like the way I look, or the way I talk, or he would rather hire a pretty girl 'cause he's never been laid and he figures he might get lucky if she works for him—and he won't, by the way. Then, one day, the entire economy fucking *tanks* because some greedy assholes in the United States who I've never even met before decided to gamble with other people's money and lost it all and caused a goddamn *global* recession. Yet *those* assholes get to keep their jobs and give themselves million-dollar bonuses while I can't even get a job at the goddamn mall! Then the older generation looks at you, and they're like, 'What's wrong with this kid?' because back in *their* day the unemployment rate was three percent and there were opportunities everywhere and you could throw a dart out a window and hit a fucking job—there was no competition from China or India and you could support an entire family on a single assembly-line income. Now, the price of gas and food and rent and tuition is, like, four times higher than it was before, while wages have flatlined for decades and yet they can't understand why we have such a hard time making it. All they care about is lowering their taxes so they can drive big SUVs and go on luxury cruises and live it up before they die. I mean, seriously, if they had just *told* us to get a degree in, like, human resource management or computer sciences or something like that, I would've fucking done it! Instead they coddled us, told us we were all special, and said 'follow your dreams' and 'you can be anything you want to be' so go out there and be a rock star or an actor or an astronaut and it was all fucking *bullshit*! I wish one person, just one, would've taken me aside and said, 'This is how it is. The world's different now.' So no, I don't give a shit about my ten-year reunion. I don't need to know what my friends from high school are doing because I already know the answer. They're doing nothing. They're doing fuck-all. Nobody is. Everybody knows there's a problem, everybody knows we're heading off a goddamn cliff, but they do absolutely nothing about it. I mean, I keep waiting for something, *anything*, good to happen, but . . ."

I shake my head and look down at my feet and they're burrowed into a mound of dark brown sand. Doc peers at me with a concerned look on his face for a long time before finally saying, "Shit, dude. You want a beer?"

I pause before answering, "Yeah, I'll have one."

He walks up the grassy path to the cottage, returning a minute later with two bottles of beer. He twists them open and tosses the caps into the sand and passes one to me.

"I was at a pub the other night talking to Nikki's friend," I continue, "and things got a little heavy, right? And then she asked me about the meaning of life."

"So what'd you say?"

"I told her there was no meaning. That this was all one big accident. But I've been thinking about it, and, I mean, it's true, there's no real meaning to any of this, but you can't look at it that way. You have to create *some* kind of meaning for yourself. You need something to work toward, a reason to get up in the morning, because without one . . . you'll slowly drive yourself crazy."

Doc nods, and then skips another rock across the water.

"Anyway, I've gotta get out of the city for a while," I say. "I might even move somewhere else."

"Really? What about your apartment? And school?"

"I don't think I'm gonna stay at Ryerson. Let's face it, I'm not gonna be a journalist. Nobody reads the papers anymore anyway. And as far as the apartment goes, I only have to give them two months' notice."

"But where would you go?"

"I don't know. Maybe I'll just buy a car and live in it for a while."

"Hmm. Like *The Road Warrior*."

"Exactly."

"That movie's awesome."

"I know."

"I love movies that are set in a post-apocalyptic world." Then he does an impression of the deep, authoritative voice used in old action movie trailers: "*This summer . . . in a post-apocalyptic world . . . .*"

"I think it'd be kinda fun to live in one."

"Hell yeah! You wouldn't have to do laundry anymore."

The conversation falls silent for a moment as I snuff out my cigarette in the sand.

"Hey, Doc, let me ask you something."

He takes a sip and waits for the question.

"What if I said I wanted to buy my car back?"

"What? Why? That thing's a ticking time bomb."

"I know. But I need a car and—"

"No, literally, it's gonna explode. It starts to overheat anytime you go past a hundred-and-twenty. Not to mention the brakes lock up, the cigarette lighter doesn't work, and the window's broken now, thanks to you."

"Still . . . I thought you wanted to get a new one?"

"I will. Soon. I'm trying to convince my parents to help me pay for it. I don't make enough burn money with my coffee man salary."

"Okay, so I sold it to you for a thousand—"

"Way too much, by the way."

"—and I'll give you eight hundred for it now."

Doc looks at me skeptically. "You serious?

"Yeah. I need a car. And that thing's got sentimental value."

He sighs. "Okay. Eight hundred. Deal."

We shake hands.

"Cool. Mind if I take it for a test drive?" I ask.

"What, right now?"

"Yeah. I need to clear my head."

He exhales slowly. "Alright," he says reluctantly. "I'll go get the keys. Just . . . gimme another minute here."

A few minutes later, I follow Doc across the yard and onto the gravel driveway where the Widowmaker is parked. He approaches the car and grabs onto the windshield wiper and moves it up and down, as if he were shaking its hand, saying goodbye.

"Why do you call it the Widowmaker anyway?" he asks.

"Because it's not a very intimidating car," I say with a grin.

"This isn't official until you actually *pay* me, by the way. And you've gotta drive me to the doctor sometime this week." He tosses me the keys. "You gonna be back in time for dinner?"

"I don't know. Might be a couple hours."

"Alright, well, gimme a shout if you're gonna be late."

"I can't. My phone's almost dead."

"Send a carrier pigeon then. I don't care."

As he's opening the front door to the cottage, I call out, "Hey! Thanks again for bringing me up here. If it weren't for you, I'd still be on that bench."

He stops in the doorway and exhales loudly. "What a weekend, huh?" And then, with gravitas, he adds, "But we really shook the pillars of heaven, didn't we, Reid?"

We both smile and nod in agreement. Then I toss my bag into the backseat and turn the key in the ignition and start revving the engine, just like old times. I honk the horn twice and watch Doc saunter back into the cottage as I speed out onto the open road.

THIRTY-TWO

The sun is beginning its descent into the western sky as I drive down that same country road we arrived by hours earlier. It's late in the afternoon but I still have plenty of daylight left. To be honest, I don't know where I'm going—I just want to see a bit more of the countryside and be alone behind the wheel for a while. I check the old yellow map of Ontario unfolded on the passenger seat and realize the Dockett family cottage is actually a few kilometres south of Kincardine; I decide to bypass the town entirely as I head north and the scenery is spectacular, with sweeping green fields stretching for miles in every direction. I must have caught it on the right day. Then I see row upon row of wind power generators gently spinning in unison and their calming motion puts my mind at ease.

Doc left his iPod hooked into the car radio, so I scroll through its contents and settle on a song called "Road" by Nick Drake. His wistful voice and soft acoustic guitar blend perfectly with the surroundings. I'm surprised Doc listens to such gentle music. Perhaps I've underestimated the man. When I arrive in the town of Port Elgin, I take a turn toward the waterfront and follow a winding road running north along the edge of the lake and the sunset over the water is absolutely beautiful. The sun looks bigger, redder and brighter than I've ever seen it before, and it divides the sky into four distinct colours: blue, orange, pink and purple. I park the car beside a giant flagpole and lean against the hood feeling awestruck by the sight.

Part of me wishes I could stay in one of these small towns and live a more pastoral life. Seeing a sunset like this every night would be amazing. But how could I afford it? Where would I work? How do these communities manage to survive if all the young people are moving away? How could I make friends, see movies, go out on dates, if there are no other people my age? It would be impossible. Best not to think about it. For now, I'll just admire the view.

I stare out at the multi-coloured sky and I'm suddenly reminded of the three goth-hippie girls and their spoken word festival—the one I promised to attend. I get back in the car and pull my phone out of my backpack and turn it on. The battery is flashing red, so I waste no time in dialing Craig's number.

"Hello?" he answers.

"Craig, my battery's about to die, so I can't talk for long. How'd it go last night?"

"Man, I slept with a nineteen-year-old! She was born in the nineties! She doesn't even remember Reagan!"

"Well done. So what're you doing tonight?"

"No plans yet. Why?"

"Wanna do me a favour?"

"Hmm. Depends. What is it?"

"There's a show going on in Kensington Market. I told them I'd go but I can't, so I need you to tell these three girls I'm sorry."

"Who're the girls?"

"They're goth-hippies."

"What kind of show?"

"Spoken word."

"What's that?"

"It's butt-fucking poetry."

". . . I don't know if I wanna go to *that*."

"Come on. Take your teenage girlfriend with you."

"Maybe. I might. The girls—what're their names?"

"Swan, Dive and Hype."

Craig is silent.

"So, yeah, can you tell them I'm sorry?"

"Where the hell are you anyways?"

"Doc's cottage. I'll call you when I'm back."

"When will that be?"

"No idea."

"Ugh, fine. . . . I'll try to swing by."

"Thanks, man. Appreciate it. Talk to you soon."

I hang up the phone as the battery beeps twice and the screen slowly fades to black. Then I toss the dead phone onto the passenger seat and recline in my chair, taking a brief moment to relax, reflect and witness the sun's final descent into the horizon. The sunlight shines directly through the windshield forcing me to squint my eyes and I can feel myself gradually drifting off, succumbing to my daydreams. And then, inadvertently, I fall fast asleep.

THIRTY-THREE

I was anxiously pacing around the hotel room with a cigarette in one hand and a cellphone in the other. I didn't sleep at all the night before, having tossed and turned until 7:30AM. I was only twenty-three years old, but I knew exactly what I wanted. I was so tired of drifting from place to place under the guise of "travelling." I wasn't really travelling at all. I was running. It was time to stop. I wanted to go home and stay there for good. I had to make the call.

The hotel was mere miles away from where Rachael was living. A few months earlier, she suggested we spend the Christmas holidays together—she even said she would come meet me wherever I was. We were about to make the arrangements, but I ultimately declined without giving her a reason. The truth is, I wasn't ready to see her. I was embarrassed by who I'd let myself become and I needed more time to get my life in order. Now it was January, and I'd come to find her again. I was finally home.

I dialed the number, heard her voice on the other end of the line, and asked her to meet me in a café downtown we used to go to. She was happy to hear I was in town, but she already had plans; I eventually convinced her to cancel them and see me instead. Then I hung up the phone and stood in front of the mirror and practiced everything I had been too afraid to say: how I felt about her since day one, how I kept thinking about her no matter where I was, how sorry I was for being so callous and how I would try to make it up to her in the future. My plan was to get a job, any job, and stay there with her—if she'd have me.

The weather was cold and damp that night and the roads and sidewalks were covered in muddy slush. I trudged through the rain and snow and it soaked into my shoes. The café was a fifteen-minute walk from the hotel and I passed the time by listening to sappy music on my iPod. Even now, I can clearly remember the uneasy feeling in my chest and the butterflies in my stomach. My heart was racing and I couldn't wait to see her.

Nobody was in the café when I arrived, save for the one old woman behind the counter. I ordered a hot chocolate and she poured it into a big, white mug and then I sat down in a booth in the corner and kept an eye on the entrance. Every time I heard the door chime, I nervously expected to see her face coming in through the doorway, and I was always disappointed when I saw it wasn't her.

So I waited. And waited. I checked my watch: she was ten minutes late. Then twenty. Then thirty. The place was closing in an hour. Where was she? I had to order another hot chocolate because my mug was long empty. I continued to wait. She'll be here soon, I thought. She's on her way now. The woman behind the counter began to sweep the floor and told me they'd be closing in ten minutes. Then she dimmed the lights and turned off the window sign. I stayed there in the booth, hoping Rachael would walk in before they closed for the night, but she never did.

I continued to wait in front of the café as the owner locked the doors, expecting to run into Rachael on the street. I refused to admit it, but deep down, I knew she wasn't coming. I stayed there and waited until my face and hands became so cold that I had no choice but to slowly withdraw back to the hotel.

I was sitting at the foot of the bed with a bottle of gin in my hand trying to call her, but I could only reach her voicemail. I didn't leave a message. I never found out why she didn't come that night, but I already knew the answer: I was too late. She had waited for me for a long, long time and I always let her down. I left the following morning and began planning my move to Toronto. Six months later she was gone, and I drank heavily every single day. Then the blackouts started.

THIRTY-FOUR

"Come on!" I shout, slamming my fist against the steering wheel. I'm driving south along the same country road heading back to the cottage when the car's engine begins to sputter and emit a dark black smoke. It coughs and rattles for almost a minute until I have no choice but to pull over. Smoke continues to bellow out through the gaps in the hood even after the car has stopped; I get out and try to lift the hood but the metal is too hot and I can't see anything in the darkness. I try to start it again and the interior lights flicker, but the engine stays silent. The Widowmaker is dead.

A green sign tells me Kincardine Avenue is only five hundred metres away, so I grab my backpack and say goodbye to the car, abandoning it on the side of the road. I cross a bridge over the Penetangore River and see another sign advertising a bed-and-breakfast in town two kilometres to my right. There's an empty police station and a few houses in the distance, but the road is dead quiet. I follow it alone in the dark, afraid I might run into a bear or a pack of wild coyotes. Eventually I pass an old gas station and a boarded-up restaurant before arriving at the bottom of Queen Street—the main street in Kincardine according to my map. Around the corner I find two or three motels and when I enter one I'm greeted by a friendly middle-aged woman behind a desk. I inquire about using the phone and she gasps and asks about my eye. I lie and tell her it's from a sports injury. She offers to help me cover up the wound and I say, "Yes, please," so she leads to me into the bathroom and applies a concealer which manages to hide nearly everything but the swelling. I thank her as we go back into the lobby where she passes me a landline phone. I call Doc twice, but he doesn't pick up, so I leave a message on his voicemail telling him I'm going to spend the night in town and try to get the car fixed in the morning.

Overhearing my story, the woman sympathizes with me and only charges me the weekday rate instead of the more expensive weekend rate. I thank her again, and as I'm handing her my credit card I ask if she knows a good mechanic in town. She tells me about a guy named Gerry while marking his location on my map. Finally, I ask one more question about restaurants in the area and she recommends I follow the main street. "There are some nice places up the hill from here," she says.

I take the key and head over to my room. Inside there are white walls and blue curtains and it has all the usual amenities. I throw my backpack on the bed and decide to head downtown in search of food. It's a longer walk than I expected; I pass through a residential area and over another bridge until I reach the top of a hill where I'm greeted by picturesque streets with tiled sidewalks and old-fashioned lampposts. Out of curiosity, I veer off the street and follow a gravel path downhill toward the water as it curls around the river and under a bridge and past an old light-house. There's a sign above the door that reads *1880*—I assume that's the year it was built. I continue along the path until I come to a small marina with boats docked across the river to my left. The path extends to a long, narrow pier, and at the end of the pier there's an orange-and-white sign—some kind of nautical marker. I sit on the concrete base of the sign and gaze out at the lake using my car key to scratch my name into the metal while whistling a harmonica solo from a song I can't remember.

When I finish carving my name, I overhear someone to my left and glance across the water to see a girl standing alone on another dock about twenty or thirty yards away. She looks like a mirage, like she's floating, and she has a cute, flipped bob haircut and wears a loose, navy blue sweater. I watch her for a moment as she sits down at the edge of the dock and her legs dangle over the side. I desperately want to talk to her; I'm trying to think of something to call out, but nothing comes to mind.

"Anna! Come on! We're going!" somebody shouts from behind her. She stands up from the dock, dusts herself off, and gracefully runs off to meet them, disappearing without so much as seeing me.

Still in a stupor, I stagger back along the gravel path and up the hill onto the street, continuing to wander aimlessly until I eventually find a crowded pub with live music. I have no intention of getting drunk—in fact, I'm deathly afraid of alcohol right now—but I just want to eat, relax and kill some time before I go back to the motel.

I walk inside and the room is filled with loud, jovial people of all ages. A thirty-something musician with short hair and a generic, radio-friendly voice is playing cover songs on an acoustic guitar, mostly popular sing-alongs and classic Irish tunes. The bar counter is long and L-shaped and I find an empty stool at the far end next to a map of England hanging on the wall. The young guy sitting beside me drinks a red cosmopolitan and doesn't say a single word to anyone the entire night. I order a beer and a glass of water and quietly keep to myself, listening to the music and taking in the surroundings.

About ten minutes later an older woman across the bar asks me why I'm all alone on a Sunday night. I tell her I'm from out of town and she says I should have a nice young lady on my arm, promising to help me find one. I smile and nod and raise my glass to her. Tomorrow I'll get the car fixed, I tell myself. But tonight I won't worry about it.

Sometime around one o'clock in the morning the bartender rings a bell to announce last call. I prepare to settle my tab and as I'm fetching my credit card from my wallet I see her coming in through the door—it's Anna, the girl from the dock. This time she's accompanied by a friend, a blonde woman who appears to be a few years older.

For the last song of the night the musician plays a surprisingly good rendition of "Lola" by The Kinks. The crowd recognizes it from the first chord, and they immediately break into a drunken chorus; I grin in spite of myself and quietly sing along with them. I watch Anna and her friend buy two bottles of beer before moving to the front of the stage and shouting "La-la-la-la-LO-la!" along with the musician. During the verses they mumble the words and laugh, unsure of the lyrics. It's cute.

Suddenly I feel a tap on my shoulder and turn to see a short, heavy-set girl with straight black hair and a tight blue dress. She speaks with an East Coast accent and says, "Hey, we're having a bonfire party on the beach after the bar closes, if you wanna come?" I look over at Anna again and she and her friend are singing "I'm not the world's most masculine man . . ."

"Yeah, sure," I say. "Just let me know when you're leaving."

She introduces herself as Tammy and then she smiles and walks away. I finish my beer and place the bottle on the counter and then nervously approach the stage. I keep my eyes focused on the musician as I sidle up beside Anna. When the song ends, everybody in the audience claps and cheers and then the noise gradually subsides; seizing the opportunity, I turn to Anna as if I'm noticing her for the first time and her eyes are big and bright.

"Hey, did you hear about that beach party?" I ask, figuring it to be a safe place to start. When she looks at me, her expression moves suddenly from joy to concern.

"Whoa! What happened to your eye?" She leans in close to inspect it and says, "Here," while pressing the cold end of her bottle against the wound. "You should ice that down."

"Thanks." I completely forgot about the black eye; apparently it's still somewhat visible through the make-up.

"How'd this happen?" she asks.

"I got punched in the face."

"Why? What'd you do?"

"I threw a pylon at a guy. It was for a good reason though."

She laughs. "Some people! Well I hope he looks worse."

"Oh, he does."

"You've gotta be more careful!" She pulls the bottle away from my face and says with a grin, "Nope! Still swollen!"

"So, about that beach party—"

"Oh yeah. We're going. Are you?" I nod and she says, "Cool. My name's Anna."

"Ethan." I shake her hand.

"And this is my cousin, Emily." She motions to her friend and I shake her hand too.

"I'm guessing you're not from around here," I say.

"Nope! We're from Perth. Do you know it? It's a small town outside of Ottawa. We're here on vacation. What about you?"

"I live in Toronto, but I drove out here with a friend of mine."

"Ah, a city boy! That's cool. Well, let's grab another round and get going."

"I think they already did last call. . . ."

"Oh it's no problem." She whistles at the bartender currently fiddling with the cash register. "Hey! Tim! Can we get three more?" He gives her a quick nod and retrieves three bottles of beer from the fridge below. She pays him in cash and hands one to me. I'm impressed. "Alright, lead the way!"

The three of us follow Tammy and a band of locals down to a sandy beach at the southern end of town. It's hard to see in the darkness and the moon is new, but, unlike in the city, there's barely any light pollution, so the stars are shining brighter than I've ever seen them before. I walk carefully, navigating by listening to the voices in front of me, eventually arriving at a fire pit where logs have been arranged in a circle around a pile of ash. Tammy asks us to gather some firewood;

Anna and I are given a flashlight and we go off on our own in search of branches. I find a shrub with some skinny twigs and start breaking them off.

"Where did you grow up?" she asks.

"Hard to say. I moved around a lot as a kid. By the time I was seventeen I had already been to ten different schools."

"Yikes. You're a nomad."

I laugh. "Basically. So I don't really have a hometown. Not anymore anyway."

"Why'd you move so much? Were you an army brat?"

"Nope. My parents just . . . liked moving. And then they divorced, so I was constantly being shuffled back and forth between them."

"Well, you definitely weren't raised in the country," she says, pointing at the twigs in my hand. "Those'll never light! We need something bigger."

"Sure they will!"

"Nah, we've gotta keep going. Come on!" She grabs me by the hand and leads me further down the beach. Then we look up at the stars and I try to impress her with my knowledge of the constellations. Unfortunately I only know the Big Dipper, but I take a shot at a few others.

"See that line of stars over there?" I say, holding up her arm and pointing at a section of the sky. "Those three right there? That's Orion's Belt."

"Are you *sure*?" she asks skeptically.

I pause a long time. "No," I finally say.

We both start laughing as she jokingly pushes me away. Eventually we find a dead tree hanging over the edge of the beach and strip it for branches, victoriously returning to the fire pit with long pieces of wood held across our arms. Sadly, they've already gathered enough wood to get the fire started and the fire is huge, burning over four feet in the air. Anna and I look at each other and laugh again, dumping the excess wood to the side.

The two of us sit together on one of the logs just as Tammy starts passing around a bottle of Jack Daniels. The musician from the bar has joined us too, and he's strumming instrumentals on his guitar while Anna and I talk about our lives back home. She tells me she plays guitar too, and writes songs in her spare time.

"Do you play in a band?" I ask.

"Nope, by myself. I haven't played any of my songs in front of people, though, 'cause they aren't quite ready. But I've started recording."

"That's cool. I used to play together with my friends, but I haven't done that in a long time."

"What kinda stuff would you play?"

"We did a lot of punk rock, mostly."

She puts her hands to her mouth to amplify the sound and says, "Boooo!"

"What, no good?"

"No! You should be playing folk music."

"Hey, I like folk! *Blood on the Tracks* is one of my favourite records. And I love Neil Young. My old man used to put his albums on all the time. I can sorta play the harmonica too."

"Really? You should've brought one!"

"Yeah, I should've. But I didn't know I'd be at a bonfire at two in the morning."

"You gotta be prepared, man! But yeah, so folk music, I saw this guy named Harry Manx play at this place in Gatineau a few months back and it was amazing. Do you know him?"

"No."

"He plays the slide guitar. It's so good."

"Cool. I'll check him out."

She smiles and everything falls silent.

"So, why'd you stop playing?" she asks.

"Ah, I got distracted with school and work and everything else. I mean, I realized I couldn't make a career out of it, so it just didn't seem all that important anymore."

Anna looks at me and blinks a few times before saying, with absolute sincerity, "I can't imagine anything *more* important."

"Maybe you're right."

"Of course I'm right! When you come visit me in Perth, we'll jam together. Here." She retrieves a pen from her pocket, removes the cap with her teeth, and then grabs my left wrist and begins scribbling her email address and phone number across my forearm. The pen digs deep into the skin and I try not to wince from the pain as she goes over each letter a second time. By the time she's finished my entire arm is etched in black ink.

"There," she says.

"How long are you in town for anyway?"

"We're leaving tomorrow morning. Going back to Perth for a couple days and then me and Emily are driving out to California."

"Really? What for?"

"Just to check it out. I've never been to the West Coast before or seen the Pacific Ocean. We're gonna go surfing and mountain biking. It's gonna be great. You should meet us out there."

"Hmm. I don't know if I can."

"It won't cost much."

"It's not that."

"Why? Can't get time off work?"

"No, I'm still looking for a job."

"So how do you pay the bills?"

"I've got a credit card and some savings."

"Huh. And what're you gonna do when your savings run out?"

I shrug my shoulders. "Party's over, I guess."

She reflects for a moment and then says, "Well then you should definitely meet us out there."

"I don't know. I've still got a lot of things to sort out back home. And my car is kinda dead. . . ."

As I'm talking, the bottle of Jack Daniels is passed to me and I examine the label a moment. Instinctively, I want to take advantage of the free alcohol and drink as much as possible, but after last night I'm afraid, worried I might get horribly drunk and embarrass myself again.

"Speaking of which, it's getting late," I say as I pass the bottle to Anna. "I've gotta get up early and find a mechanic. I should probably get going—"

"You're gonna leave us? Already?"

"I've got your phone number. I'll call you."

Anna stares straight into my eyes and then holds onto my arm and rests her head against my shoulder. "Come on, Ethan. *Stay.*"

I don't think anyone has ever asked me to stay before. Ever. In my entire life. People usually express some mild regret that I'm leaving, but they never put up a fight. Her emphasis on the word is mesmerizing. *Stay.*

"You said you like Neil Young, right?" she asks, beckoning the musician across the fire to let her borrow his guitar. After strumming a few chords, she begins to play a song I don't recognize, a song about childhood memories, and it feels as if she's speaking directly to me. Her voice is like a whisper—it's subtle and understated and haunting, and the lyrics conjure various images of the past. She sings about going to the fair, falling in love, becoming an angry adolescent, smoking that first cigarette and wanting to be alone—the gradual descent into adulthood. It makes me realize how much I miss my family, my friends, and feeling young and optimistic about the world.

The song stays with me. I hear it over and over again in my mind as Anna and I wander along the beach until the sun begins to rise. She's light-footed and graceful, guiding me along through the sand and over the rocks and hills. We visit other bonfires and greet the locals and search for more firewood in the tall grass to keep the fires burning throughout the night. Stripping down to our underwear, a few of us go swimming in the shallow lake and the water is warm and calm in the darkness. All of my worries and concerns about the car and money and Natalie seem to vanish and all that matters is the moment. Moments like these are what it's all about. The day-to-day experience will always be a grind for me, but every once in a while I have a moment where everything feels okay, where I feel at peace. It might only happen once a week, a month, a year, and it may only last a few seconds, but they do happen, usually when I'm least expecting it. Those moments, however brief, those are the ones worth waiting for.

It's the early morning and Emily, Anna and I are walking across a parking lot underneath an orange sky. Our hair is wet and we're carrying our shoes in our hands and a van full of people is waiting for them at the other end of the lot. Emily waves good-bye and runs off ahead of us so we can have a moment alone.

"Do you need a ride?" Anna asks.

"No, it's okay. I can walk."

"You sure?"

"Yeah."

She hugs me tightly and holds onto me for a long time. "Take care," she whispers. "And come see us in California."

"I will."

"Hopefully your eye heals up by then," she says with a smile. Then she kisses me on the cheek and turns around and jogs toward the van. The door closes and the engine hums and they drive away down the street and out of sight. I stand there dripping wet, holding my shoes, and then I look up at the morning sky and breathe it all in.

Soon I find myself back inside my motel room, writing all of her information down in a notebook. I run a bath and soak in the tub and relive the entire night in my mind, staring down at the ink on my forearm and wondering if I'll ever see her again.

THIRTY-FIVE

Today, I don't know what to do. I'm lying beneath the blankets, staring at the white ceiling with a few hours to go before I have to check-out of the motel. There's no hangover, no headache, no stomach pain, but my car is still stalled on the side of a road two kilometres away. I walk to the lobby and try calling Doc again, but he still doesn't answer, so I look through the phonebook and try to find a tow truck driver who can drag my car to a mechanic. Before making the call, though, I figure I should try to start it one more time. I put on a change of clothes, throw my backpack over my shoulder, and retrace my steps from the previous night along Kincardine Avenue. Soon I'm alone in the countryside again, and the Widowmaker is parked right where I left it.

I unlock the door, toss my backpack inside and put the key in the ignition. I look upward and send a silent prayer to no one in particular, then turn the key and step on the gas. The motor sputters and whines. It screeches loudly. And then, to my surprise, it suddenly relaxes and settles into a sustained hum. I thank whoever answered my prayer, then shift it into gear and slowly press down on the pedal. The car moves sluggishly off the shoulder onto the road. The engine is shaking violently, but as soon I push it past sixty everything runs smoothly again. "Woo-hoo!" I shout, patting the dashboard to congratulate her for a job well done. I soon realize, however, that when I hit the brakes the engine begins to stall. I reapply the gas and push it past sixty and it runs normally again.

The mechanic marked on my map is only a few kilometers away. I drive down the country road, careful to keep my speed above sixty until I spot the garage. There are two broken cars on display on the front lawn and the place looks vacant. I pull into the parking lot and the car jerks to a complete stop. I walk into the garage and meet Gerry, an amicable old guy wearing a dusty grey jumper. He's relaxing on a chair and reading a newspaper when he notices me. "Good morning! What can I do for you?"

"Gerry, right? How's it going?"

"Good! How're you doin'?

"Not so good. My car's fucked up."

"It is, huh? What's wrong with it?"

"Well, the engine keeps smoking for starters. It runs fine if I'm going over sixty, but any slower than that and it chugs and stalls."

"So you've gotta keep it above sixty, eh?"

"Yeah."

"Kinda like that movie *Speed*?"

". . . I suppose."

"And you're like Sandra Bullock? Drivin' that bus?"

"Well, yeah."

"I've always wondered what that'd be like, y'know? Drivin' a big bus? Anyhow, I don't know much about Cavaliers, to be honest with you. I'm more of a Ford guy. But bring her in here and I'll see what I can do."

The car shakes and fumes as I slowly drive it into the garage. Gerry tells me, "It might be a while, but we've got some newspapers and magazines over there. Can I get you a cup of coffee?"

"No thanks, I'm good. But is there a phone around here I can use?"

"Yup, there's a phone booth outside. You need change?"

"No, I should be alright."

The booth at the side of the garage has seen better days: the door is broken, the paint is peeling off, and the yellow phone book attached by a chain has been soaked in rain and snow, rendering the pages virtually illegible. I pick up the receiver and listen to the automated voice system, surprised to learn that phone calls now cost more than a quarter, especially long distance calls. I grudgingly swipe my credit card through the yellow slot and dial a number—one I wrote in my notebook before I left the cottage. The phone rings four times before a recording answers: *Hey! Natalie here. I'm sorry I can't come to the phone right now, but if you leave your name and number, I'll get back to you real soon. Thanks!*

I haven't thought about what I'm going to say. Any of it. And so it all pours out, unfiltered, from the moment I hear the beep:

"Hey, Natalie. This is Ethan. I'm sorry for calling you so early, but I kinda figured I'd get your voicemail anyway, so . . . I'm actually stranded in Kincardine right now, believe it or not. Jeff and I drove out here yesterday and then my car broke down, so now I'm stuck—oh, and I'm calling you from a pay phone, so if it cuts out, that's why. Anyway, I just wanted to say I'm really sorry about what happened the other night. I don't know why I get like that. I think I'm just . . . angry at myself for things that happened a long time ago and, for whatever reason, sometimes it just comes out. But it had nothing to do with you. I, uh . . ." I exhale and shake my head, trying to find the words. "I don't know . . . I guess I kinda push people away, y'know, when it feels like they're getting too close. It's easier that way. It's . . . it's easier to be alone, to stay detached, to keep everybody at arm's length and leave them before they leave you. But I don't wanna do that anymore. . . .

"Anyway, I really liked spending time with you. I mean, I don't know what I want, but the truth is, I don't even worry about that stuff when I'm with you. So, if you'll let me, I'd love to make it up to you sometime. My friend was telling me about this coffee shop on Bloor where they have, like, a thousand different board games, so we could check that out. Or I could come see your band play again sometime. Anyway, that's it. Call me when you get the chance, okay? Take care, Natalie."

I hang up the phone and stare vacantly at the receiver. Not the most eloquent message I've ever left, but, for once in my life, I was being sincere.

THIRTY-SIX

"How long have you owned this car?" Gerry asks. We're standing in the garage and his arms are crossed and he appears to be agitated.

"Actually, I bought it yesterday."

"From who?"

"A friend of mine."

"Well, let me tell you something. This friend of yours? He treated this car like a piece of shit!"

"Really?"

"Yeah! The oil was way down. We're talkin' bone dry here. The brake fluid. The transmission fluid. Christ, even the *wiper* fluid was empty. And look at these spark plugs!" He shows me a handful of small metal cylinders covered in black gunk.

"Looks bad."

"Oh it's bad. Not to mention she's leaking oil all over the damn place."

"Can you patch her up?"

"I can try. But my God, do me a favour and tell that friend of yours to never, ever own a vehicle again, would ya?"

"I will."

Within two hours Gerry has the Widowmaker working properly again. I hand him a credit card and we wait for the machine to print out a bill.

"So where you off to now?" he asks.

"Well, I've gotta drive my friend back to Toronto, but after that?" I pause a moment. "Say, if you could go anywhere, where would you go?"

"Someplace warm probably! It's great here in the summer, but wait 'til winter rolls around, I tell ya. I'd rather be at an all-inclusive resort somewhere, kicking my feet up and drinking margaritas all day long."

"I hear ya." He passes me a receipt and I sign it. "Thanks, Gerry. Have a good summer."

"You too! Safe travels. Hope she runs well for ya."

I get in the car and drive down the road, leaving Gerry and his garage behind. The engine is running smoothly with no hiccups and no shaking. I fill up at a gas station and then stop at the first intersection I come across—there's no traffic and the radio is off and the air is silent. All I hear is the hum of the engine and I notice my knees aren't aching anymore. The day is young. Another beautiful day and it's not even noon yet.

I idle at the intersection while I think back to all the people I met over the weekend: Charlie, Swan, Sofia, Anna. Each of them tried to tell me something. People have given me advice before, but they're all just words, and they all fade, eventually. I continue to live my life through trial and error, sometimes not recognizing the error until it's too late. Ultimately, the question I struggle with most is: What am I supposed to do with my time here? In other words: What's important to me? A career? Earning money? Family and friends? Love? Do I stay in one place and try to build something, or do I travel the world and live out of a suitcase? Do I live solely in the present, or focus on creating a future? Time is the most valuable thing we have, and I'm so afraid of squandering it. So now I ask myself: What should I do?

My phone is dead. The gas tank is full. And come tomorrow there's nowhere I have to go, nowhere I need to be. It's a freedom most people will never know. I may be running out of time and money, but, right now, the past doesn't matter. Neither does the future. It's only the moment. A clean slate.

The town of Kincardine is in my rearview mirror. I think about the beaches and the bonfires and the lighthouse at the edge of the river and the pristine waters. It's a shame I have to leave this place, but I'm overwhelmed by the curiosity, the sense of wonderment and intrigue of what else is out there for me to find. One day, when this is all over, I'll return to Toronto and build a real life: get a decent job, start a career, form long-lasting relationships. I might even hang some paintings on the walls. But for now, all I have is a map and an open road. An entire continent to explore. And I'm ready.

Epilogue

It's the end of February and the snow is falling. I spent the rest of the previous summer journeying across Canada. It's a beautiful country; all my life I've driven down its roads, lived in its suburbs, but never saw it for what it really was. For weeks I explored the small towns, parked my car on gravel shoulders and walked through forests of majestic trees, swam in freshwater creeks and daydreamed in the warmth of the sun. I'll never be able to describe what I saw and felt and experienced to another human being—those memories are mine and mine alone.

In Northern Ontario I went to visit one of the towns I lived in when I was a kid, a blip on the map called Onaping Falls. I hadn't been there in fifteen years, yet the place seemed to resist time; the stores and houses looked exactly as they had in my dreams, although a few were boarded up, discarded and forgotten. I strayed from the highway to walk along the river and stand where A.Y. Jackson painted alone in the wilderness nearly a century ago, and the surrounding trees loomed larger and seemed more confining than they had in the past.

When I arrived at my old house I was surprised to find nothing more than a pile of brown dirt and ash and debris. The property had been completely levelled; I stood beside my car and stared at the mound of dust feeling oddly relieved. Then everything became clear and at that moment I finally understood: I rooted through my backpack and found Rachael's postcard and placed it atop the rubble. I didn't need it anymore. I didn't need an old piece of paper or a photograph to remember her by. I thought I could forget about her, that I could burn away all the memories, but she was with me wherever I went. Always. She changed my life. She continues to change my life. She taught me so much. And I feel so happy, grateful and fortunate to have known her.

Anna and I sent emails back and forth while we were both on the road. I would go to internet cafés and login to my email account and there would be pictures of her mountain biking or hiking in the desert. I was seriously considering driving all the way to California until I heard she had met someone during her tour of the Grand Canyon. He immediately introduced her to his parents and then proposed a few weeks later. She said yes. They've already set a date. So it goes.

I returned to Toronto and paid Doc what I owed him for the car, which he used to buy a plane ticket to South Korea. He left a few days ago. I'm thinking about following his example and dropping out of school too; I want to leave this city and drive south, far over the border, someplace where it's always warm and the waters are crystal blue. I want to experience a world I can see and smell and touch.

Natalie never called me back. It's been over seven months and I still haven't heard from her. I don't blame her. Our mutual friends don't really talk anymore either. I'm not even sure if she heard the message I left on her machine. One night I dreamt she snuck a pack of guitar strings into my mail slot, but that was just a dream. Now, anytime my phone rings, I eagerly check the display, hoping to see her name, but it's never her. Maybe hope isn't enough. I've been hoping for a lot of things to happen for a long time. Maybe it takes more than hope.

Craig recently started dating a girl named Alicia who is a few years older than we are. I've met her a few times and I think they're great for each other. He also formed a band in which he sings and plays rhythm guitar and they rehearse at least twice a week. Between band practice and his new girlfriend I hardly see Craig anymore, but I'm happy for him.

Thankfully, I haven't had a blackout since July. I tried quitting alcohol cold turkey, but I couldn't do it. Didn't have the willpower. And I couldn't stand being with my friends when I was sober. Now, whenever I meet up with them, I moderate myself by drinking no more than what's in my hip flask—usually less than six ounces. I severely water down my drinks, too, and nobody seems to notice. There's been a relapse or two, nights when I drank more than I should, but certainly not on a daily basis and nothing like before.

These days I find myself in coffee shops more often than bars. I bring a laptop or a pad of paper and write for hours, usually until they kick me out at closing time. It's not much, but it gives me some small sense of purpose—a reason to get up in the morning. In retrospect, I think part of the reason I drank so much was because I didn't have a routine. Alcoholics need a stable routine and a preoccupation to keep them busy. I didn't work hard enough because I didn't know what I wanted. Now, I have something to work toward. I want to be a writer. Someday.

An alcoholic support group often meets at one of the cafés I frequent, and sometimes I can't help but overhear their conversations. They talk about their struggles and why they want to stay sober and their words often strike a chord with me. I want to walk over to them, talk to them, share my experiences, but I wouldn't know what to say. I never know what to say.

At that same café, there's a girl behind the counter who pours my tea and takes my money and she has a soft voice and a gentle smile. During our exchanges, in the brief moments we have together, I want to initiate a conversation, but I don't know where to start. The fearlessness I used to have, that confidence brought on by inebriation, is long gone. I still haven't figured out how to function in the real world without it. But I will. Eventually. It's like learning how to walk again after years of being stranded out in space.

Everything I've written here is true. Mostly. Granted, the names have been changed, the characters are generally composites of two or more people, the locations are not always exact and the chronological order has been altered, but everything in the book actually happened. I did meet a fisherman at a bar and ask him to play "Hey Jude." I was denied a spoon because of heroin usage in the bathroom. The teacher who was cheating on her husband? That exchange happened, word-for-word. I snorted cocaine, took ecstasy and extracted codeine from painkillers. I recklessly abused alcohol on a daily basis for over seven years. I did get into a fight with a homeless man over three dollars. Then I shared a slice of pizza with the next panhandler. He still hasn't won the lotto yet. A waitress did accuse me of eating chili peppers and chugging vinegar to impress a girl. Another bartender told me I passed out in an alcove and the staff had to pour water on my face to wake me up. I did chug a bottle of tequila and fall asleep in someone else's apartment. I did tell that forty-year-old man in the blazer to fuck off. The police did blame me for kicking over mailboxes. I did get punched in the face by a Korean guy for trying to throw a pylon onto a roof. My friend really did get distracted by a guy eating a jar of mayo. I did drive to Turkey Point; I swam in the lake and helped them lift that house frame and then drank at a bar with the locals. I did witness a fire outside of Bathurst Station. I did have an argument over the phone with a prostitute who wanted to go to law school. A girl did tell me that atheism is a turn-off. I did run into three girls who were building a model cathedral outside a church while I was high on codeine and they asked me what my *real* name was. The interviewer at the coffee shop did tell me to cut the bullshit. The guy who looked like John Lennon really did tell that calculator story. I did get advice from a man in his forties who warned me about the midlife crisis. My car did break down on a country road and I had to keep it above sixty kilometres per hour or the engine would stall. My friend and I really did sneak into an elementary school and play with the gym equipment. We also had that conversation on the pier. I did wait in a café for a girl who never came. I was in love with her for over ten years. I did meet another girl at a small town pub and we built a bonfire by the water and she wrote on my arm. We still keep in touch.

I'm not telling you this because I'm proud of what happened. I can't condone my behaviour or offer you an explanation for addiction. It's just something that some of us deal with, especially in this day and age when so many people are struggling. Long-term substance abuse ruins nearly every cell in your body. My brain is irrevocably damaged. My liver is no doubt fat and inflamed. There are scars everywhere—you can see it in my eyes and in my face. I've lost friends and family and people I cared about. I've lost everything. But my heart is still beating, pushing, moving me forward. It's the search that keeps me going—the search for that sense of fulfillment that comes so easily to some, but eludes so many. It's what gives my life meaning, and my life will have meaning for as long as I keep looking.

To tell you the truth, I'm not sure why I wrote all this down. The process didn't feel particularly cathartic. I think I was just tired of the phoniness, the inauthenticity of it all. I've never recognized myself in any of the characters I've seen in books or movies or on television. They never talk like me or my friends or the people I know, nor do they deal with the same problems and concerns. I wanted to write something real, something true, in the hopes that there were other people out there like me who had lived through something similar. I wanted to let them know that, in spite of everything, I was still alive. Because none of us are truly alone. I'm gradually learning how to see past all the little things, to just live and breathe, and accept whatever may come as we wander through this land of the blind.